THE

GIRL

IN

DULUTH

Sigrid Brown

Paperback ISBN: 978-0-578-33876-7
ebook ISBN: 978-0-578-33877-4

Library of Congress LCCN: 2021924471

Book design by Jess LaGreca, Mayfly Design

For Cynthia

ONE

Visitors sometimes feel uneasy in the county I grew up in. They call it a strange and lonely spot. The kind of place where something terrible might happen to you but no one would ever know exactly what, because they would never be able to find you.

Those of us who grew up in the county see it differently, of course. When someone goes missing, we know where to look.

Four years ago, when I was eighteen, something awful did happen there. A whole sequence of events had led up to it. It began months before, or you could even say years.

I hate to be melodramatic, but in order to tell it right, here we go: it was a clear, bright day in January, but a storm was rolling in.

TWO

"The rapids first, don't you think?" I said.

I climbed up into Frank's truck and slammed the door. Obediently, he began driving east. In the bright lavender sky was a growing softness from the snow beginning to come down.

But in Frank's eyes was a sharpening alarm. He was hunched over peering upwards through the foggy glass. I straightened up and clutched my own hands primly in my lap. It was certainly not in my long-term plans to look as old and wrecked as Frank did when *I* reached forty-three.

We took the two-lane Highway 400 out of Aulneau to Hartnell Rapids. Tonya liked to bring picnics out there in the summer and fall. She said the noise of the rushing water replaced all the thoughts in her head and made her feel as if she were something wild.

Snow was filling in the crevices of the big gray-black rocks. They looked as if they had been dabbed with paint. The lines of white made the rocks look even bigger and blacker. Dark pine trees arrowed up to the sky while the other trees, bare of leaves, were crowned with soft clouds of whitish-gray. The overall effect was like a black-and-white photograph.

Tonya would have liked it—but she wasn't there to see it.

It was now after four. The sun would be down within the hour. Frank turned around in the small dirt lot, switched his lights on, and drove the eight miles back to town.

We passed the population sign, 1,047—a lower number than it had been when they changed the sign two or three years before. Then we were coming up to the apartment above the feed store where I lived with Tonya. I looked at the small front window, where I had left a lamp turned on. I pressed my forehead into the cold glass and sighed.

We didn't stop, but drove on through.

I didn't particularly love that apartment. Just an hour before, I had been looking around it while doing calculus problems and sighing for a different reason.

The bathroom door with its broken hinge leaning against the wall. It had been haphazardly replaced with a yellow polyester curtain nailed over the doorway. The old industrial carpet: rough, clay-colored fuzz that looked filthy no matter how often I vacuumed it. Mine and Tonya's single beds across from one another in the one small room.

I was about to call my best friend Zee to see if she'd come over and add some brightness and beauty to the place. We might bake some cookies and scent the stale air with cloves and cinnamon.

Then I heard a slow tread on the stairs that came up from the street. Soon the faint sound of Frank's knuckles trailing over the door.

He was a tall man with a stoop. That and an imploring expression made him seem as if he were always slightly ashamed of himself.

Many times Frank had come to our place knocking weakly like that. Usually he would train his desperate look on Tonya. Once he'd come begging her to shoot a dog for him. His own poor dog, which he'd accidentally run over when he was drunk.

Today, Frank had a favor to ask of me.

3

His eyes were gray. The dark brown hair on his big, triangular head was going that way, too. He sighed, leaned against the refrigerator, and coughed his wet and dirty smoker's cough, his chest caved in, but the top of his eyes still glittering on me.

"She's your mother, June," he said.

I shook my head and affected a laugh. Tonya my mother? Only in the strictest biological sense . . .

I turned to the stove to heat water up for tea. It was January, after all. It was northern Minnesota, so it was cold out. Not morbidly cold, but cold enough. Twelve or fifteen degrees.

And it was almost three. The sun was getting low. On every episode of *Father Brown* or *Miss Marple* that I'd ever watched, characters in mystifying situations almost always suggested that tea might be in order, to bring about some calm and clear some heads. And often at these times, the light in their cottage, or village rectory, or stylish London flat, looked like this—slanting through the windows and tinted with blue or gold.

I looked out the front window of the shabby apartment. A rusted pickup drove slowly by on Highway 400. Dirty snow was banked up on either side. A light was turned on in one of the small frame houses across the street.

Yes, there was gold in the sky, though clouds were moving in.

I could imagine better tea companions than Frank, my mother's unfathomable choice for a longtime best friend.

"Tea, Frank?" I asked him politely, nonetheless.

"Juney," he said.

I poured hot water into my beautiful white teapot. A curly handle, an embossed diamond pattern around the rim. On the front a cluster of blue flowers, on the bottom a unicorn and the words "Blue Rose." This summer I had bought it at the annual church basement sale at Sacred Heart.

"What have you got there now?" Tonya had said, and laughed gently, when she saw my new pot. "You are such an old lady,

June." I didn't know if I liked that better or worse than her usual, "You're such a weirdo, June."

"She called you? Where is she?" I asked Frank today.

He shook his head. After a second, I shook mine back at him. Until Tonya called to ask for help, she didn't want to be found.

I shrugged and Frank said, "I'm worried, June."

"Why?"

"With how crazy she drives?"

"She's driving?" I put down my cup.

"Must be. Her car's not here."

"It's not at your place?"

Frank shook his head. My mother had had her license taken away multiple times, one of those being a week or two ago. As far as I knew, she hadn't gotten it back yet. She liked to speed and spin out on the ice and whip around corners as if she were in Nascar.

"Well, call Jack. See if he's got her," I said.

The perpetual sadness in Frank's downturned, hound-dog eyes dimmed into something harder. Jack was one of the cops in our town.

"No," he said.

"When did you last hear from her?"

"Three days ago. And we check in every day."

I frowned.

"And you haven't heard from her," Frank added.

"That doesn't mean anything." I took a sip of the honeyed orange tea to see if it would sweeten away my bitterness and calm me down. It didn't, but I pretended the magic was real by swatting my hand as airily as a Southern belle who had grown up surrounded by protection and love.

"Three days ... That's nothing ... Don't you remember when she disappeared to Winnipeg for a month?" I said.

"You got a postcard. I remember you did."

"And Christmas. She wasn't even here for Christmas." Tonya had been gone for at least two weeks this past month, right over the holiday. She never even gave me a present.

And when New Year's arrived, she didn't have money for the rent, either. Today was the 11th and we hadn't paid it yet. Luckily, our landlord felt sorry for me. She was letting my mother's negligence slide for a while, as she'd had to do a hundred times before.

"Frank, what's up?" He began to look uneasy then. I tried to inspect his gloomy eyes and he flicked them away. He looked down and began to knead the fingers on one of his hands as if they were frozen and he had to rub them back to life.

He said, "Sometimes people—do things."

"What? What things?"

"Well." Frank was still squeezing his fingers one by one and looking at the ground.

"What people? You don't mean like," I said slowly, "you don't mean like those women on the news?"

"What women?"

Frank looked up at me squinting. The women who had gone missing, I told him, sitting up straighter at the table. He must have heard about it. It had been on TV a few nights ago. The station was doing an investigative report about it. Five women had gone missing from northern Minnesota this year. Three had been found murdered, one of them just a few days ago. The other two were still gone.

Britta had been talking about it, too. She was my boss—the editor at our county's newspaper.

"The women in Duluth," I said. "You think something like that happened to Mom?"

Frank shook his head. He blinked a few times. "Duluth? What? No."

"They were her age." Three of the women had been in their late thirties and early forties—Tonya was thirty-nine.

My hand began to shake. I put both hands on my knees. I stopped drinking my tea.

"Frank?"

"No. Nothing like that. What I meant was . . ." Frank shook his head again and trailed off.

"Listen—maybe we really should call Jack."

"Juney . . ." Frank came from his post at the refrigerator and stood in front of me. He sat down at the table and looked at me helplessly.

"What?" I said.

"Juney . . . please . . . Now, don't get all excited about what you saw on the news. There's all kinds of things on the news. None of it has anything to do with this. Who said anything about Duluth?" He lowered his eyes.

I stared at him. "It makes sense."

"I don't know about that. What I'm saying is—" Frank sighed. "Listen, Juney. That's not what I meant."

"Then what?"

"She hasn't been herself lately."

I stared at him for a moment. Then I nodded slowly.

Frank was right. My hippy-dippy mother, laidback and charming, happy-go-lucky, had been anxious recently. Excited sometimes; at other times nervous.

For a while now. Since the late fall, at least—around the end of November. When she came back home after a few weeks of being away.

Then at Christmas, she had left again. When she came back after this second trip, she had at first seemed more relaxed. I conjectured that perhaps she'd had a wondrous spiritual experience out in a snowbank or talking to a random weirdo in a backwoods bar somewhere.

But her peaceful feeling seemed to fade. In a few days, she was upset again.

She'd snapped at me when I asked her, "Hey, Mom, what's

with you?" I used "Mom" when I felt like annoying her. As long as I could remember, she'd always liked it better when I called her "Tonya."

"Leave it alone, June." She was sitting on the edge of my rocking chair, her head in her hands, at the time. Her voice low but harsh.

Which wasn't like her. Tonya had never been attentive or solicitous. She'd never seemed particularly interested in being my mother at all. But while she might tease me sometimes, she was rarely bad-tempered or cruel.

Later, she'd apologized: "I'm sorry, Juney. It's just that I'm in a little bit of a jam—moneywise. But I'll figure something out. I always do."

It was true. My mother always got us by on the odd jobs she did sporadically around the county: gardening, shoveling snow, yard work. Occasionally she rebuilt old furniture she found at the dump and drove it down to an antique store in Lisbeth. She cobbled together enough for the bills at some point.

Better late than never—which must also have been the mantra of our landlord and the gas company.

No—not herself at all. A day or two after she'd barked at me, Tonya had even taken a job at Otten's, the big flooring factory in Gabekana, forty-five miles away. She hadn't held a steady job there, or anywhere, for years.

What had prompted her to do that, after all this time?

Unsurprisingly, she was only able to keep the job a few days.

"So, what? You think she killed herself?" I said crudely.

Frank winced. I thought of how Tonya had once said to me—when was it, just a month or two ago?—that when she died, she wanted to be cremated, not buried.

And she didn't want her ashes locked up anywhere. Not in the ground. Not in an urn or a box.

"Or a teapot," she'd added with a little smile.

I reminded myself now that people did that: planned ahead.

Even young and middle-aged people. They knew death was always waiting and could come at any time.

But Tonya? Tonya, who rarely committed to anything more than an hour in advance? Tonya, who groaned, "Oh, just a little longer, Juney," when I pulled her out of bed at eight-forty on a day she was due to be out by nine?

Frank tugged at a tuft of his gray-brown moustache and began to turn his head restlessly around the room. He looked at the rickety wooden rocking chair by the door and the tall brass lamp wobbling beside it—both of them my own treasures, snagged on one of Tonya's dump trips.

Then Frank moved his gaze to the eastern window with the torn screen. He looked for a long moment at Tonya's bed. It was covered with a worn blanket, a pale spring green. Finally, his eyes settled on a stuffed animal on my own bed. The old and ratty brown dog had enormous black plastic eyes and a despondent expression. My Uncle Aaron had given it to me when I was little. I loved that dog because I loved my Uncle Aaron; the only thing I didn't like about it was that it sometimes reminded me of Frank.

"But why would she—hurt herself?" I said.

"Why?" echoed Frank. His eyes faltered and he looked away from the dog and gazed past me out the window. I glanced over my shoulder, as if I would catch a glimpse of the reason my mother might have killed herself out there on the empty street.

I looked back at Frank. "Yes—why?"

"Juney, if she's done something"—Frank's hands were now on top of his head—"if I found her like that . . . Juney. I can't do this. Not alone. If I saw her like that— I'd go out of my mind. You gotta come with me, Juney."

"What aren't you telling me?"

Frank stood up. For a moment I just sat there with my hands on the table, looking up at him.

Then I moved my eyes back down at the table. I spoke to its

Formica top in the most poised and cynical tone I could manage. That technique sometimes worked to chastise Frank into calming down.

I told him that he must not get himself all worked up. Tonya was likely just at the lake or somewhere in the woods. She had wanted to see the falls or walk out on the ice or talk to the birds. Alone. She took some back roads so Jack wouldn't see her. She was fine and would come back to us at some time or another, the way she always did.

But thoughts about her funny moods were filling my head. There were also images of dead women's frozen fingers sticking out of the snow. Women who had been killed for a reason no one seemed to know yet, then dumped like trash in the woods north of Duluth.

And then the more mundane possibilities: Tonya had gone into the ditch or hit a deer. Or the car was out of gas and her phone had gone dead quickly in the cold.

She couldn't call and there was no house close enough for her to walk to. She was in the car, trying to stay warm. Waiting for someone to come by. Her thin body shivering.

She was petite and slender, my mother. Unlike me. Though she was certainly tougher than me. I reminded myself that she had blankets, food, hats, mittens, scarves. She had a whole winter survival kit. I had put it in her trunk myself. I had even included matches. Tonya could build a fire in her sleep.

She was always running out of gas. Undoubtedly, she did it on purpose—to make her life more of an adventure. To see if she could make it where she was going before running out, and to see how she would manage to get out of her predicament if she did. She had walked to farms for help, hitched rides with semi drivers, ridden horses and tractors, spent the night in hunting cabins in the middle of the woods. She loved it. She loved coming back to town with blisters on her feet and rocks in her shoes and a twisted ankle and a sunburn. Bursting with a new story to tell.

I looked up again at Frank. He had taken out his keys and was gripping them in his hand.

No—did we really have to go to Tonya's rescue again? It was Sunday. Tomorrow was a school day, and I wasn't even finished yet with calc.

And go trolling all over the county, because she hadn't told us where she was? She might even be annoyed when we found her. I hated that: when I was with my mother and it became obvious she would rather I wasn't.

I looked outside. The first few flakes were glittering past the window.

After a while, I pushed back my chair, stood up heavily, and let out a sigh like a great gust of wind. I went to the door and dropped into the rocking chair so hard it groaned. I started to put my boots on and my tortoiseshell cat Enid came out from under my mother's bed. She got playful when I flipped one of the laces this way and that. Her little needle claw got stuck in the braid and delicately I lifted it out. She purred to thank me and jumped up into the chair.

I let her sit a minute, that lovely warm weight. I petted her short, silky fur. Half of her face was black and the other half was gold, making her eyes look as if they were slightly different shades of green. Nothing made a place cozier than a beautiful cat. I put her back down on the floor.

When she meowed indignantly, I said, "Sorry, baby. I'd like to keep sitting here, too," and shot a glare at Frank.

Frank peacefully ignored the look and came to put his coat on as well. When he started talking to my cat in the high-pitched, dopey voice he used on babies and animals, and reached down to pet her, Enid squeezed her eyes tight. Her fur practically crackled under his fingers, rough and grayish with no nails to speak of.

I heaved forward out of the chair and the cheap wood let out another grand crack. Enid dashed away and Frank watched her go, looking sadder than ever. He began to cough again and I handed him a scarf to protect his crummy polluted lungs.

"Let's get this over with," I said.

THREE

Twelve miles west of town, to Miskomin. At County 84, Frank turned right.

We drove to the beach along the narrow, pebbly road getting covered with new snow. It was now falling heavily. Frank's old windshield wipers creaked as they struggled to make a dent in it. The road felt soft and slippery under the tires of his truck and the tall, dark trees closed in on either side of us, getting nearer to the edge of the road the farther north we went.

I watched the deep ditches and the darkening woods apprehensively. I was not like my mother; I liked it better in town.

The clouds and snow were too thick now to reveal a sunset. The last of the day ended as if someone drew a dark shade down over it.

Tonya was not standing at the end of County 84 at Miskomin Beach, looking out at the frozen Tree Lake. We got out of the truck to check a ways down the shore, Frank shining his flashlight around on the rocks and trees and the tips of driftwood poking out of the snow.

Then he left me standing in the dark as he walked out on the ice. This time of year, the snow-covered lake that spread out over Canada for almost seventy miles looked like any big stretch of field in the county. It was impossible to tell precisely where the beach ended and the lake began. But starting not far out were small clusters of orange and yellow lights, a village of fish houses on the ice.

That's where Frank would be now, shining his light around carefully to watch for auger holes and gut buckets, knocking on the wooden doors and asking if anyone had seen my mother.

I hadn't wanted to go with him. In the daytime, I liked the winter lake. On a clear day, it was a dazzling blue-and-white world. Lots of families, kids packed into fat snowmobile suits, grandmothers in clodhopper boots and leather mittens passing around homemade doughnuts.

I had gone out fishing with Zee and her parents just a week before. We drove for what seemed like miles on the ice road. Zee in coveralls and aviator sunglasses wrestled a northern pike out of our hole and Zee's father cleaned and cooked it right on the ice, in a cast-iron skillet over an open fire.

Zee's cheeks got bright red in the cold. On our way home in the family truck, the color didn't fade. Her skin was as burnt from the wind as it would have been if we'd spent a sunny July afternoon at the beach.

At night, the frozen lake was a different kind of place. More men, more parties. More snowmobiles ripping drunkenly around on the ice. I could see and hear them now. Their mosquito whines, their sharp beams of white light.

I didn't love standing alone on the dark shore, either, listening for cracks in the brush.

"No," Frank said, when he came back.

After the lake, on to all of my mother's favorite meditation spots. The birch grove near Amisk Bay. The old school forest.

"Frank, should we call Jack?" I said when we came up empty. "The more people who are looking for her . . ."

Frank frowned. "If Jack finds her, then he's got to bring her in."

"I just think—Jack could probably even track her phone."

"Let's try Blueberry Hill."

She wasn't there. Before we pulled back onto 400, Frank lit a cigarette and smoked it as he drove with the window cracked.

The car got very cold before he was done. He flicked the butt out onto the snow.

Back on the highway, I sat as close as possible to the windshield to watch for the deer that with their stunned brown eyes might emerge suddenly like huffing, heaving battering rams out of the driving bits of snow. We didn't see any. Unlike us, deer weren't dumb enough to be meandering around tonight.

Frank turned again off 400, this time south on County 82. About a mile down I said, "You think she'd come down here?"

"You don't think so?"

"I didn't think she liked to."

We were coming up on the driveway to the farm my mother and my Uncle Aaron had grown up on, Uncle Aaron until he was ten, Tonya until she was my age. Their parents had died that year in a car accident. A semi hit an icy patch on Highway 400 and knocked them off the road.

Tonya, Uncle Aaron had told me, was already beginning to get wild at that point. When their parents died, there was no one to rein her in.

Uncle Aaron was sent to a suburb of Minneapolis to live with his aunt and uncle. While they asked Tonya to come, too, she wouldn't. She was eighteen. No one could legally force her to go.

Instead, she got her first job at Otten's, the factory in Gabekana. That was where she met Frank. After a year of working together in the same department, Rip and Cut, they both left.

My grandparents' ninety-acre farm went to Tonya. After several years of never paying the property taxes, she lost it.

Talking about the farm seemed to bother her. She never brought me there. Frank had taken me once, though, when he was shoeing a donkey for the family who lived there now. Like Tonya, he was a jack-of-all-trades. I was twelve or thirteen at the time. This family had a multitude of homeschooled children with white-blond hair, busy doing a whole number of things:

carrying pails of feed for chickens, grooming horses, milking goats. One was patching a tire on a tractor and a lot of them were hauling wood. A girl about nine years old came to hold the donkey for Frank when the smelly beast showed its teeth at me and I squealed and dropped the rope.

In all the commotion, it was hard to picture a teenage Tonya on the place, lounging on the wooden steps of the neat blue farmhouse in her bare feet and a halter top. Her eyes closed in the sun, probably contemplating the astral plane.

I could picture myself there, though. Big farm animals and the creepy, buggy woods—not so much. But visits to a neat vegetable garden and grandparents who, by all accounts, had been both loving and practical, I would have liked.

Like me, my grandmother had been big-boned and tall. I hadn't been able to fit into any of tiny Tonya's tight jeans or flowing hippie skirts since I was eleven years old. Not that I wanted to. Instead, I got my eager paws on some of my grandmother's belted dresses, cardigans, and button-up blouses. Uncle Aaron had managed to save them before Tonya threw them out and they fit me perfectly.

At the driveway to the farm, I thought Frank had decided I was right. He didn't pull in. I waited for him to turn around. Instead, he kept driving south.

After a mile or so, I said breathlessly, "Deer."

Frank braked slowly. We both peered ahead into the swirling black-and-white.

"Sorry." I felt silly. It was only a mailbox with a jaunty wooden pelican perched on the top.

Frank put his foot back on the gas. The truck tires whirled for a second in the soft snow before catching on the blacktop. Then we kept going.

"What are you thinking?" I said after a minute. "Where to now?"

"Well. Let's just—"

Frank kept driving, looking straight ahead. For several miles, we still saw an occasional orange or yellow light a short distance off the blacktop. We met one car, inching through the snow like an insect through heavy soil. Then no more. No more house or yardlights, either.

At a narrow gravel road marked "Minimum Maintenance," Frank turned right. It looked like a logging road.

"Really? You think she'd come in here? In the winter?"

We were heading into thick woods. Frank didn't respond as the truck bumped slowly through the snowy ruts. We got stuck in one and Frank rocked back and forth to get out. He was looking nervy again.

He coughed and said quietly, "Juney. I was really hoping we'd find her at Miskomin Beach."

He made another turn. Then another. Soon I had no idea where we were in relation to County 82. Frank coughed some more. Then he started to breathe heavily—fast, shuddering breaths. I hoped he wouldn't hyperventilate. If Frank lost it, then I'd have to be the one who got us out of here; and at the point in the storm when even more snow had fallen, and every tree and every turn looked even more like every other tree and turn than they did right now.

"Are you all right? Frank, calm down . . ."

We couldn't see more than a few yards in any direction. The darkness outside the reach of the headlights was complete and the trees, a mix of tall pines and birch, seemed to be growing right on top of one another.

"Frank, where are we? Is this where you hunt or something?"

Frank muttered something under his breath.

"What?"

Still he didn't answer. But he kept muttering to himself, in a soft but high, whimpery animal voice. And whenever he made another turn onto another road, almost always even narrower and bleaker than the one we'd been on before, he groaned and gritted his teeth.

"What is it? What's the matter, Frank?"

At one point, we saw something unexpected ahead: the headlights of another vehicle.

To me, it was a relief. A sign we were still in civilization.

But not to Frank. He swore. Then he stopped in the middle of the road.

"Frank—what are you doing?"

Frank's whimper grew louder.

"Pull over and let him get by," I said. "There's not enough room."

The truck drew closer. Frank kept looking at it.

"What is wrong with you? Pull *over*!"

A bright beam of green light shone from the bed of the truck out into the woods and Frank let out a long breath. Finally, he cut it out with the strange creature sounds. He gave the truck some gas and moved to the right. The other truck squeezed by.

"It's okay, Juney," he said and sighed, "it's just shiners."

"Who did you think it would be?" The news that there were shiners in the woods didn't have a calming effect on *me*. Shining deer might be legal under some circumstances, but I had always associated shining with the kind of hunter who didn't care about sensible rules, hunted out of season, carried a beer in one hand and a gun in the other, and slopped around the woods aiming a blast at every leaf that quaked.

Frank scowled at the truck as it passed. "Stupid. In this weather?"

He started driving again. I watched him.

"Who did you think it would be?" I asked him again.

Frank shifted in his seat, rolling his shoulders. He sniffed and wiped his nose with his fist. "Your mother. I hoped it was your mother."

"You about shit yourself because you thought it was Tonya?" I frowned, not at Frank's incompetent lie, but at my own lapse into language he would understand. The problem was, vulgarity made him more comfortable.

"Well. Now you're just seeing things, Juney," he said with a greasy grin.

"Frank. Tell me the truth. Do you and Tonya sell drugs? Is that what this is about?"

It wasn't the first time I'd considered this not unlikely possibility. For a few years now, Tonya hadn't made a secret of the fact that she and Frank smoked pot. I often found her skunky stashes around the house.

It would explain how she—usually—managed to make the rent. It could explain Frank's panic now. Did Tonya owe someone money? Was this "someone" after her?

I'd asked Frank, and Tonya, about selling drugs before. I wasn't surprised at the answer. They were probably afraid that if they told me the truth, I'd turn them into the police. Who knows—maybe I would have.

"No. Of course not, Juney . . ."

We had gone only about a mile more when Frank pulled over again. He turned off the engine and sat looking out his window, breathing deeply.

I glanced around. What a surprise—trees. Snow.

"What's this? Why here?"

Frank was quiet. He put his hands on his knees and looked down at them. After another long moment, he said, "June. Maybe it's time we headed back."

"What are you talking about?" I looked at him. "Why?"

Frank only continued to sit very still in his seat.

"You came here for some reason. You think Mom's here?"

Frank lifted his hand from his lap. He rested it on the key in the ignition.

"I'm calling Jack." As I went to pull my phone out of my coat pocket, I felt Frank turn to look at me.

"Don't," he said.

I looked at him, surprised. Frank's pleading tone had been replaced with a firmer one.

I looked down at my phone. "Well. It doesn't matter. I'm not getting a signal anyway. Are you?"

Frank didn't move to get his phone. "No."

"How do you know? Check it."

"I don't want Jack to find her," Frank said slowly. "I'll find her. And I want you to stay in the truck."

After a moment, he closed his eyes. He took his hand off the ignition and put it on the door handle. He exhaled and I watched him.

"You don't want Jack to find her? Why in the world not? Frank? What if she's hurt? Jack could get her to town much faster than we could. He could even meet us on 400. If you think she might be here, let's go look. And get your phone out and see if you're getting a signal."

"Just give me a minute." Frank's eyes were still closed.

We sat for a few seconds in silence. Then I grabbed Frank's flashlight. I opened my door.

"June," Frank said, his voice as sharp as it ever got, "listen to me. Don't, now."

I left the passenger door open and crossed the road through the truck's headlights. Then I walked towards the woods. The wind was very cold on my face. The driving snow even colder.

"This way?" I called.

"June! Come on and get back in the truck." I heard his door open and shut. I hadn't gotten very far by the time he caught up. I was wading through the deep snow in the ditch. The thick tangle of brush on the edge of the woods was bent heavily under the snow. I did not see an easy way to crack and break my way through it. No trail.

I began to try to make one. When a branch snagged the pom-pom on my hat and pulled it off, the wind seemed to whistle through one ear and out the other. I swept the flashlight beam on the ground until I found the hat and without even shaking it jerked it back on. A terrible cascade of snow slipped past my collar and rippled down my back.

Frank was hovering just behind me. Once he reached out to tug on the back of my coat. I shook him off.

"Don't." He was back to begging. "June. You don't want to—"

"This way?" It wasn't long before I found out for myself.

The trees were growing very close together here; but then there was a small clearing. I beamed the flashlight into the middle of it and through the heavy flakes falling in the bright yellow light, I saw her. Her long brown hair on the snow.

FOUR

Officer Jack Laverne was looking at me with the same polite interest and concern in his dark blue eyes that they'd had since he was plain old Jack Laverne, three years ahead of me in school and helping me with *Julius Caesar*.

"Did you try looking up the word?" he would ask patiently, whenever I complained that I didn't know what a portent was, or that Mark Antony's speech made no sense at all because everyone knew that ambition was a good thing.

Jack was an inch or so taller now than he had been when he was in school. Though at six feet he had been tall even then, taking jump shots as shooting guard on the basketball team and always looking just as serious and intense about the baskets that he landed as he did about the ones that he missed.

He had filled out, too. He looked like an adult now. Though his face was still almost pretty, with his long lashes and curly brown hair.

We were still friends. I didn't see Jack as often as I had in our small school, only about twenty or thirty kids in each grade. But he always stopped his cruiser to say hello whenever he passed Zee and me walking through the parking lot at the grocery store, or noticed Zee's '99 Chevy Cavalier parked at the gas station near the river. It had a couple of red booths to sit in and a Hot Stuff Pizza.

Tonight, I looked at Jack across the small table in the Aulneau police station. An interview room. A plain, blond wood table and nothing on the walls. Filling the room was a smell faintly reminiscent of a wet farm animal. My gray wool pea coat was dripping on a hook near the door.

I realized that I knew this scene. In fact, this whole succession of scenes. I'd seen it a thousand times on detective shows.

Someone's missing. There's a search—and inevitably a body turns up. The police get involved. Interviews are conducted. Jack was the police, though it was still hard sometimes to think of him that way.

As long as I didn't directly relate my procedural TV knowledge to my own role in this moment, my own voice, my own body sitting in this chair, I knew exactly what came next.

Jack the police officer would ask me what had happened. What I had seen.

Could I answer? Was my head filled with useful details? Could I speak? I had no idea what I could and couldn't do.

I was here. My feet were on the ground.

At least it seemed that way. But was it Earth under my feet? Was I alive, or dead myself? Or had I been beamed to some other place?

A place where the wildly unthinkable could happen. The kind of place where a person who was part of your everyday, whose being and presence existed even when she wasn't in the room, a person who was walking and talking one minute— could, in the next, simply disappear.

I couldn't have said for sure!

The Jack I had known for years asked, "How are you doing, June?"

I shook my head.

"I think—I should be crying," I said finally.

"No. June. There's nothing you 'should' be doing. Everyone—"

"I guess so. Should I be surprised?" I thought, for an unnerving second, that I was going to laugh. I felt so strange!

"June?"

"I'm not sure that I am. Surprised . . ."

"Okay," Jack said slowly. "What makes you say that?"

That was Jack the police officer speaking. I looked at him in his dark blue uniform.

"Is Tonya really dead?" I asked him.

Jack tipped his head slightly to one side. His blue eyes filled now with pity. That frightened me. I felt like an abandoned dog on the side of the road.

"Yes, June," Jack said.

"And you have her now."

"Yes," he said gently.

"Will I have to identify her?"

"No. Not unless you want to. Your uncle—"

"I don't think I do."

"That's fine."

"Jack," I said, "I think there were plenty of times when I thought we might find Tonya dead."

"Okay."

"It's different, though—that she's actually dead."

"I know."

Jack's father had died of a heart attack when he was still in school; Jack was fourteen or fifteen at the time. Since then, it had been just Jack and his mother in their yellow farmhouse near Lund, a ghost town about five miles west of Aulneau with one boarded-up general store. Jack helped to take care of his mother's horses and the three or four beef cattle they raised there.

"You do know," I said, and he nodded.

I nodded, too. "It's always been like this. Do you know what I mean, Jack? She gets lost. She calls to say she thinks there's a cougar tracking her in the woods. She tries to tell me where she is—so I'll be able to find what's left of her. 'You know, June— by the Kraus's old place.' No. I don't know. Or you call me, Jack—you say she's run her car into the ditch. I'm waiting for you to say it: 'She's gone.' But it doesn't happen. She gets lucky. She gets out of it every time. Because"—all of the sudden I was speaking breathlessly—"because, Jack, she wants to live. Tonya loves to live. So she claws her way out. She loves to experience things. Be outside. Be in the woods. Be in the middle of it all. See and do things. Jack. That's what I mean—this is different. Tonight. Not just because . . . Listen. What I'm trying to say is—I always thought that at any minute she might be out there getting herself killed. But the last thing I was ever worried about was that she'd kill herself."

Jack opened his mouth to say something. I talked over him.

"But what am I supposed to think now? Was it all, like, what do they call it—a death wish? Was this, like—the greatest adventure or something? *Death*?" My voice shook on the word. I waited. I almost ached for it. Still, I didn't cry.

A light went on in Jack's dark eyes. He nodded thoughtfully.

"How else can you explain it?" I could feel my voice rising.

"Was she worried about anything, June?"

"Yes." I waited to get my breath back before I finished. "Money."

"Right." Jack made a note on a notepad. I watched him.

"She had to quit her job," I said. "When she started at Otten's after Christmas . . . I don't know why she went there. She didn't say. I didn't want to ask. I kind of didn't want to jinx it. You know? I guess she had finally gotten tired of piecing stuff together. Getting a little money here and a little there? Right? She must have."

For just a moment, those few days after Christmas, I had been hopeful. Stupid! I had thought maybe things were going to be different. Tonya had made the decision that finally she was going to get herself together. Settle down and provide a steady living. Be a real mother. She was nearly forty, after all. Maybe her approaching birthday had been enough to rattle her into shape.

Then she blew it. When Otten's didn't work out, maybe she got depressed?

It didn't seem realistic, though, if I were being honest with myself.

Why now? When I had just turned eighteen? When at any time now she could have simply said she wanted me out of her life for good and kicked me out of the house.

"Or maybe," I said, the caustic laugh finally escaping, "she just thought that if she did herself in following the right Yuletide ritual or something, she'd end up on the astral plane with Persephone and the Buddha."

As soon as I said it, I felt a little sick. I was grateful when Jack said, "Tell me about your mother's money problems."

I sat back in my chair, crossed my arms, and waited for the nausea to pass. I gave Jack a look that was probably harder than was strictly necessary. "She had to quit at Otten's."

"Why?"

"Because of you."

"Because of the reckless driving citation. And not her first one," Jack corrected me, with an insufferable level of gentleness.

I sighed and nodded. "That's right."

"Driving wasn't her only option for getting to work, June. She could have joined a carpool."

"I know." I had said this to her myself.

"Did you know she had a handgun?"

"No. So it is hers?"

"Yes. Registered in her name."

"Where did she get it? When?"

"Last month here in town. Right before Christmas. Can you think of any reason she might have wanted a gun?"

"Other than to kill herself?"

Jack held on to his impassive expression. "Was she scared of anyone?"

"Not that I know of." I looked at him closely. "Why do you ask?"

"Did she go anywhere recently?" He wrote something down on a yellow pad. "Any trips?"

I told Jack about Tonya disappearing over Christmas. "It wasn't unusual. But she was gone for a long time in November, too." Jack nodded and kept writing.

"Do you think that means something?" I asked him.

He put down his pen. "I need to show you something."

There was a plastic baggie with a piece of paper in it next to him on the table. He pushed the bag towards me.

"Is that your mother's handwriting?"

It was a note written in blue ink on a piece of notebook paper. The big, loopy script ran slantwise across the lines.

"Do not be sad. Do not be afraid," it read. "Death is the ultimate voyage to the unknown. I am full of love and light. Look for me in the stars. Do not look for me in my body. I am not there!"

Then her name. Her full name: Tonya Elizabeth Bergeron.

My eyes blurred for a second. The blue letters seemed to slide around on the page.

"June." Jack seemed to be shouting at me from down a mountain. "Are you all right?"

"What?" I pushed my chair away from the table. "Yes. Fine."

"Are you going to be sick? If you need to go to the bathroom—"

"No." I kept staring at the note from the safer vantage point of a foot away. Jack began to pull the bag back to his side of the table. I reached out and put my hand over his to stop him.

Jack let go of the bag. Quickly he wrapped my fingers in his. His hand was warm.

I looked up at him in surprise. For just an instant, I caught a tender look on his face. Then he jerked his hand away from mine as if it were a hot stove or something disgusting. He grasped for his pen instead, and sent it rolling across the table.

I kept looking at him. Jack and I had never been the touchy-feely kind of friends. I couldn't remember him ever doing something like that before.

He was bent over his pad now, writing hard enough that his dark curls quivered faintly around his ears. I got the feeling he wasn't going to look up until I spoke.

Had I really seen what I thought I had?

Zee wouldn't have been surprised by the moment at all. She had been saying for months that she thought Jack was "after me." I thought it was ridiculous. We were just kids to Jack.

But Zee called Jack a real creep. A cop hovering close by a high-school girl, waiting for the precise moment she graduated so he could snatch her up?

"You're crazy. That is *not* what's happening," I always said.

I liked to hear her talk about it, though. It was strange to think of Jack in that way, but it was also flattering. And having a cop in love with you would have its perks. It would lend you a tint of respectability, a fine thing when you didn't get a glimmer of that from your home or your closest relations.

Plus, the scenario of young men finding a way to charm high-school girls into sticking around after they graduated, before they had a chance to consider other possibilities, was probably one of the only reasons our town was still alive. It happened fairly often around here.

"Not to us," Zee always said.

I watched Jack in the police station, still bent over his work.

Was Zee right? Or had Jack just acted rashly in a sympathetic moment? Was he worrying now that I might have gotten the wrong idea?

I scooted my chair forward and studied the blue letters.

"Where was it?" I asked him.

Finally, Jack looked up, his expression calm and professional again. "In her pocket."

"It's her handwriting," I said slowly. "And it's exactly what she would say."

"All right."

"She doesn't usually write her whole name out like that, though. She just does her initials. Like this." I took a piece of scratch paper from a pile on the table and picked up a second pen lying next to it. My fingers trembled. I managed to imitate Tonya's signature: a big "T," a slightly smaller "R," a bump for the beginning of the "a." Then a swooping line: "Like a long 'similar' symbol. See?"

Jack looked down at the paper, then up again at me.

"Like in geometry." I wrote my mother's signature again. It gave me an eerie feeling. I looked up at Jack. He wasn't looking very closely at what I was writing.

"Okay. But have you ever seen her write out her full name before?" he said.

"Well." I shrugged. "Yes. She had two signatures. She would do it that way"—I pointed to the note—"for official stuff. Tax forms and things like that."

"And it looked like this?"

"Yeah. But"—I tapped the signatures I'd written—"this was how she usually did it. Even checks. You can look that up. And all her letters. Poems. She's got notebooks at the apartment. You can look at those. But there's something else, too, Jack. Tonya didn't like writing with a pen."

Jack nodded politely. "She preferred working on the computer?"

I shook my head and squinted at him. He wasn't getting this at all. "No—Tonya? She hated computers. But she also didn't like pens. Ink. She liked to be able to erase whatever she'd started to say. Or forget she'd ever started. You know? Pencils. She liked pencils."

"Okay."

"And erasers . . ."

"But maybe she only had a pen with her in her car?"

"But why would she have had one? When she hated writing in pen?" As I said it, I sighed. I heard his question before he even asked it.

"Do you think you could have left a pen in her car sometime?" The careful, diplomatic tone he might have used to reason with a belligerent drunk girl who wouldn't blow into his breathalyzer.

I frowned. As much as Tonya hated pens, I loved them, particularly the smooth and liquidy blue gel type that had been used to pen this note.

"But for this? Even Tonya would have planned for this. For the last thing she ever wrote in her life?"

Of course, maybe it was a symbol. The last thing she wrote could never be erased. Tonya loved symbols and signs and "messages to and from the universe."

"Juney, send a message out to the universe," she'd say, whenever I talked about a difficult test I had coming up, or was having trouble making up my mind whether to go to college or to stay in town and keep working for the paper, or couldn't find my curling iron.

"I'm not saying she didn't write it," I said to Jack. "I'm just saying . . ."

Jack let me pause. Then he said, "What?"

"Why is 'afraid' underlined? That seems like it must mean something. Doesn't it?"

"Like what?"

"You're the cop. I'm just pointing out the clues."

Jack gave me a sharp look. I returned it. We stared at each other for a moment like that. We listened to my soggy coat drip-dripping on the tile floor.

Finally, Jack said, "What are you saying, June?"

I shrugged. "Is it possible she didn't buy that gun to commit suicide?"

"Anything's possible. But why, then?"

"Maybe to protect herself?"

"From who?"

"A drug dealer or something?"

"Was your mother dealing drugs?"

"I don't know. But couldn't she have been? To make money? She was always looking for money."

"Did you ever see drugs at the house?"

"Well"—what could it matter now?—"yes."

Jack was taking more notes. He asked me what kind of drugs and how much and I told him I thought it was only pot. I told him how for years Tonya and Frank and their whacko friend Ruby, who roasted like a buttered chicken in a tanning bed all day and carried a flask with a skull on it in her purse, had liked to party in the apartment, the three of them sitting or sprawled on Tonya's bed in a riot of laughter and smoke while I, twenty feet away on my own bed, faced the wall with my earbuds in and tried to focus on French pronouns or quadratic equations.

I told Jack how often, in the middle of the night, I'd wake up to the click of the door. Tonya would be slipping either in or out. Sometimes I'd hear a car pull up outside. Tonya's voice and other voices, too. I might recognize them as Frank, Ruby, other friends. Other times they were strangers. Sometimes Tonya came back up after only a few minutes. Other times, she didn't.

"Maybe she owed somebody money? She bought the gun before she went somewhere over Christmas, because she was afraid there might be trouble about something? Listen, Jack," I said. "One thing I'm surprised about. Tonya didn't like guns."

"Okay."

"I mean, she did know how to shoot one, though."

"Did she learn recently?"

"Oh, no. Her dad taught her." I told him about Frank coming over about his dog. By the time she got there to put it down,

Tonya said the poor animal was screaming like a rabbit being torn up by a fox.

"And she did it," Jack said. "She shot the dog?"

"Of course. What else could she do?"

"It surprises you, though, that she would have used a gun to kill herself."

"Well. Yes. I guess I could see her more—the rapids or something. Something with nature. A gun—" I shook my head. I asked suddenly, "Have you talked to Frank?"

"Right." Jack sat back in his chair and crossed his long legs. "Tell me about Frank."

"What about him?"

"Tell me what happened when he showed up at your house."

I talked about that briefly. Then my mind jumped ahead. To how Frank had reacted when we found her. To what my mother's death had looked like in the woods.

Not like her. Not even like a real person at all.

I had seen two dead people before, at funerals. One a man my mother gardened for, the other my friend Zee's grandmother. I had known both of them only a little. Both were old. And both of them, in their coffins, had looked about as I remembered them, and much as if they were just asleep.

Tonya, on the other hand—

I told Jack that I couldn't see her face. She was on her knees, slumped forward. Wearing her long red coat and a matching stocking hat. The hat had a cap of snow on it. More was piled on her collar.

Her dark hair covering her features. Her hair was so long—it hung all the way down to the middle of her back when she was standing—that the brushy, untrimmed tips were already getting buried in the new snow.

More of an image or an object, than a real human being in three dimensions. In the yellow spotlight of the flashlight, the blackness of the night around her. Like a puppet someone had tossed on the floor.

The gun was still in her hand. I stopped several feet away.

Frank ran forward, then crumpled to his knees at her side. I expected him to start moaning again like an animal. Instead, he was very quiet.

I closed my eyes when he touched her. Her hand, the one that wasn't holding the gun, wouldn't move when Frank tried to clasp it. She'd been dead for long enough that her body had either gone stiff or had frozen.

So still!

The night—the night, on the other hand, was fierce. The wind seemed to be blowing the snow in at least two different directions at once.

Tonya loved wild weather. Loved storms. But in the middle of this one, my mother, who often liked to pretend, in a strong wind, that she was a tree swaying in the breeze, her arms and hands flapping, knelt there as solid as a stone.

"And after you found your mother," Jack asked me, "what did Frank do?"

"Do?" I squinted at him.

After a moment I told Jack about Frank carefully brushing the snow from my mother's head. Not long after that, something seemed to hit him. Some realization?

"What realization?"

"I don't know."

Jack made a note on his pad. "So then what happened?"

Frank had gotten up and come towards me. He motioned back through the woods towards the road.

"Come on, Juney." His face was streaked with tears; but his voice was resolute. "Let's get back to the truck."

"What?" I stared at him. Without looking at my mother I said, "We're just going to leave her here?"

Frank stared back at me, wiping his face with his gloved hand. He glanced at my mother over his shoulder. When he turned back to me, his eyes were wet.

He pulled his keys out of his pocket and held them out to me.

"You go. I'll stay with her," he said.

Panic rose in my throat. "Frank, I don't know where we are. And I can't drive a stick."

"You what?" Frank was still holding out the keys. His fingers trembled and they jingled. "Your mother never taught you?"

I shook my head. A blistering comment rose to my mind about how I could count on one hand the number of things Tonya had taught me. The hot words faded quickly from my brain as if the cold wind had swept them away.

"I never taught you?" Frank crinkled his eyes. He put the hand with the keys in it to his forehead.

He had tried. At fourteen or fifteen, out on the back gravel roads somewhere west of town in Frank's rickety pickup, I had quickly lost interest in trying to figure out when I had to press in the clutch and when I didn't. Frank was patient.

After a few fruitless lessons, I told him to forget it. I wasn't exactly planning on driving any race cars or farm machinery.

In the snowy woods, Frank had that helpless sadness in his eyes again.

"I'm sorry, Juney," he said.

I had a physical reaction then that seemed to come out of nowhere. My legs felt weak. A memory was coming to me: Tonya and Frank taking me out somewhere in this area when I was about eight. They showed me how to cook scrambled eggs over a campfire. I detested the whole excursion, especially the mosquitoes and the horse flies, and having to pick ants out of the runny eggs before I could eat them.

Frank eating from his plate without looking for ants first. Grinning at me when I screamed at him in disgust.

Out in the woods again with Frank, my mother behind him, as still as concrete, her red hat and dark hair already speckled again with snow, I felt dizzy and dropped to my knees.

The snow was soft, cold, nice. I thought I might stay here a while.

Frank let me sit. My legs got very cold. I could barely feel them when finally he pulled me to my feet and guided me back through the trees.

Then in the truck again. Frank putting the engine in gear. Moving slowly forward through the thick snow. It was still coming down hard.

"This is better, June. Yeah. I wasn't thinking . . ."

"Thinking what?" I was beginning to come out of my "spell."

Frank looked as if he were trying to work something out. Finally, he said, "I wouldn't have wanted you driving back through the storm like this."

In the police station, Jack said, "And then what did he do?"

"We came back to town," I said slowly. "Frank drove back. Then we came here."

"You didn't try to call from there?"

"My phone wasn't getting a signal until we were close to the highway."

"Right. What about Frank's phone?"

I shrugged. "Probably not. I should have called when I got a signal."

"It's okay, June."

"But Frank didn't want me to."

"Wait," said Jack. "Why not?"

"He hates you. You know that."

Jack frowned. "He didn't want to call me, or he didn't want to call the police?"

"It's the same thing, right?"

"Is it?"

"He was mad that you gave all those tickets to Tonya." Frank

35

was also not keen on Jack because of how many times Jack had hauled him in on a drunk-and-disorderly. He preferred Randy, the sheriff, who, more often than not when Frank was out raving on the sidewalk outside of the Muni or the Legion, simply hauled him home and tucked him into bed. The two of them were the same age and had gone to school together.

Jack was taking a lot of notes. "What is it? What are you thinking?" I said.

I told him the rest of it: what it was like when Frank and I were driving out of the woods.

At first, Frank had seemed to be navigating that maze of narrow gravel roads as expertly as he had when we were driving in.

But after a few minutes, something changed. He seemed not to know where he was. Or how to get out of the woods. He stopped and looked around a few times. Made a turn, then backed up and made another. Turned around and went back the way he had come.

"I think once we drove in a square. Ended up at the same spot we started in. I'm really pretty sure that we did," I said.

"Do you think he was lost? Confused in the storm?"

"It *looked* that way. He never said so."

"Maybe he just didn't want you to worry?"

I shrugged and told Jack it was just that Frank had seemed to know the roads so well when we were coming in. As well as he knew every other back road in this county.

"Were you worried?" Jack said. "Were you afraid?"

"Of being lost?"

"Of—anything."

I looked at him for a second.

"Of Frank?" I said.

Jack kept a neutral look on his face. "Like I said, of anything."

"Why would I be afraid of Frank?"

Jack seemed to fight with himself. Then he said, "He led you to her body, June."

"Wait a minute—only after going to a million other places. And it kind of seemed like he didn't even want to go there—the place where we found her."

Jack leaned forward. "How do you mean?"

I described the way that Frank, after we turned off County 82 into the deep woods, had seemed reluctant to make each and every one of the turns that eventually led to my mother. The sounds he made, the expression on his face—as if a demon were making him do it.

"A demon," said Jack.

"Stop it. Don't write that down. You think he knows something?"

"I don't know. That's why I'm asking."

"Yes, but—Jack. It was suicide, wasn't it?"

The thought I'd had just a flicker of earlier was now searing its way into my cold-feeling insides. Was it possible my mother hadn't killed herself? That she hadn't willingly abandoned me again—for good this time?

And was that scenario better or worse?

I said, "You can't think that Frank—"

"Do you know if Frank and your mother had gotten involved—romantically, I mean?"

"No."

"You're sure?"

"I can't imagine it."

"But Frank—"

"Oh, yes," I said meaningfully.

"I'd marry her, Juney," Frank had said to me in the parking lot of the grocery store, when I was twelve or thirteen. We'd gone there to get soup for Tonya when she had the flu. "I'd marry her in a minute if she'd let me. Then I'd take care of both of you."

The words had a false ring to them, like phrases Frank was repeating after having heard them on a Hallmark special.

But there was no doubting Frank's genuine love and desire for my mother. It was all over his face every time he looked at her.

"Tonya didn't feel that way about Frank," I told Jack.

"Was she involved with anyone else?"

"Not that I know of." Despite all the wild parties Tonya and Frank were always going on about, Tonya had always acted rather nunlike when it came to romantic attachments. She didn't talk about men—or women, for that matter—or make any comments about finding anyone good-looking. She talked about people's souls and auras *ad nauseum*. But I couldn't remember a time she'd ever mentioned anyone's strong shoulders or attractive eyes. If she had boyfriends, I never met them.

Frank seemed happy with that. He didn't bring any dates around, either.

"All right." Jack made a note.

"If you're thinking Frank had something to do with this, though . . . really, Jack. That would be so hard to believe. He loved her. He couldn't have."

Jack frowned. "You did say you thought Frank was hiding something."

"Are you thinking he wanted me to witness him 'finding' her?"

"Do you think it's possible?"

"Frank's no actor. He freaked out when he saw her like that. And he's a terrible liar, too."

"He's lied to you before?"

I mimicked Frank's mawkish tones: "'Your mother loves you in her own way, June.'"

Jack looked at me for a long moment. Then he put down his pen and pushed back from the table.

He said, "June, are you getting tired? What do you think about finishing this up tomorrow?"

I looked at him and suddenly I did feel weary. As if I'd been beaten up or drugged. I nodded.

Jack said, "I'll give you a ride home. Or," he added after a pause, carefully turning his face away as he stood up, "maybe you want to stay somewhere else tonight?"

I didn't look at him, either. I felt my face grow warm. "You mean, like—at Zee's house?"

"Sure," Jack said lightly, taking his coat down from the hook next to mine. "Like at Zee's house."

His voice sounded a little funny when he said Zee's name. I watched him until he glanced my way again. Then I got up and went for my own coat.

Jack reached out with his long arm to grab it first. Instead of handing it to me, he held it aloft like a chivalrous knight. I turned around and let him help me into the clammy sleeves. The whole ordeal felt strange. I didn't really like it.

"I'll call her. But I don't mind walking. It's only a few blocks." Suddenly, I felt as if I could use a few minutes of quiet out in the cold, dark night.

Jack told me that he had already called Zee. She was waiting to hear from him again so he could tell her what to do—depending on what I wanted.

I thought about it. I decided I did want to be alone—just for a few minutes. I needed to think.

When I told Jack this, he said, politely but firmly, "I can't. June, I can't leave you alone tonight."

"I want to go home. I'll head there now. Tell her to come there. But don't call her quite yet, okay? Just give me a few minutes. Ten minutes," I begged him.

As we were walking down the hall, I heard Frank's voice. I paused a moment to look at the closed door of another room. I heard another voice that I thought was Randy's, the sheriff.

After a moment, I kept walking. Once we hit the cold air outside, a thought hit me. It gave me a final burst of energy.

I walked towards Jack's cruiser; he was opening the passenger door for me.

"Jack—her car. How did she get there? She couldn't have walked there. I guess she could have hitched to County 82, but in that storm . . . Are you thinking—that someone else must have—"

Jack didn't let me finish. "We found her car. About a quarter mile away."

"Oh."

"I'm sorry. I thought I told you that earlier."

I thought about it. Maybe he had. What was wrong with my brain?

"Why don't you go ahead and get in the car?" Jack said.

Instead, I turned and walked the four blocks to the apartment. It wasn't peaceful and quiet. The whole time I had to ignore Jack, driving doggedly along beside me.

FIVE

Why, again, had I wanted to be alone?

The apartment felt cold. I went to check the thermostat, set at 64 as usual. I turned it up. When a fresh stream of warmth came out of the radiator next to my bed, I sat there rubbing my hands over it as if it were a campfire.

I needed something to hold onto. Enid was asleep under the bed. I dragged her out as she cried and dug her claws into the ratty carpet. After petting her into submission, I buried my face in her brown-and-gold fur.

The heating bill. The electric. And rent. God. What was I going to do? Tonya hadn't even paid for January yet.

I realized that the same thing that was happening to me, had also happened to my mother. Had she felt frightened like this when her parents were killed?

She never talked about it. Even though she had lost even more than I had. Two parents who were almost always at home, who made a real living.

I thought of Uncle Aaron. He loved me, even when I was a brat to him.

But I was eighteen now. No one had to still think of me as a child and take care of me if they didn't want to.

Even if he did want to . . .

Did I want to be a burden to my uncle, as I'd always been to Tonya?

I got up and went to the front window. Jack was parked in

front of the building in his police cruiser, the engine running. I couldn't see him from this angle. But he was there, all right.

It was starting to seem possible that Zee had been right about Jack all along!

I thought about the times the three of us had spent hanging out in the school library, paging through art books together. Or chatting at the gas station. Zee loved to spin out her dreams about the future. Going to college in the city. Traveling the world and meeting every smart person she could.

And Jack? He was just as smart as Zee. He'd been the valedictorian of his class. He was always reading a book.

But he had never reveled in proving himself the way Zee and I did. Zee was flabbergasted when he didn't even take the ACT. Jack tended to zone out during Zee's lectures on racial politics and gender theory, gleaned from whatever she could find on the internet. He refrained from offering his opinions as judiciously and politely as, during his senior year, he had turned down Zee's invitation to join her newly minted Diversity Club.

Had Zee, on those days when Jack was talking about his own dreams—becoming a cop like his father, having a big family—spied him sneaking some meaningful looks at *me*?

If he *had* been looking, I'd missed it. A voice in my head whispered, "What if—*what if*—Jack wants to marry you?"

I saw suddenly that this scenario could resolve more than one uncertainty at once. Jack had a good job. While he was at work, I could decorate our house, cook and bake. I liked to do those things, actually. And I was fairly certain that once I started doing it, I'd be pretty good at sex.

I'd basically be a prostitute . . .

Because I wasn't sure I *liked* Jack—in that way.

I put Enid down on the bed and put my hands over my face. Get married, pop out a brood of Jack's kids? Before I'd done anything really fun?

So—what was I going to do instead?

I pictured myself losing this apartment and having to live out in the woods on squirrels the way Tonya probably would have loved to do. I'm sure that the primary reason she raised me in town was that when she wanted to take off for one thing or another, it was easier this way to dig up someone who was willing to stay with me. Sandy Levasseur from the feed store downstairs, who was also our benevolent landlord. Birdie and Gordon Beckel, who lived a couple houses over and across the street.

Tonya didn't have to drive me to school or arrange for one of the country buses. I had been walking to the town bus stop since kindergarten. When we got older, Zee and I often walked all the way to the school, located on a stretch of field two miles west of town.

These days, Zee usually picked me up in her Cavalier. Sometimes Tonya let me take her car, too.

I got up and turned the thermostat back down.

Then I sat down again on my bed, looking around the room.

I didn't lie down. I wanted to sleep, and yet I didn't want to.

There was my job. Yes. I calmed myself down by thinking about that. It wasn't as if I didn't have *anything*.

Every Friday afternoon, I walked from school to the office of the *North Star Herald* on Central, wrote the "School News," and typed up the coffee columns. These were handwritten accounts from old ladies who lived in outlying townships in the county. Who had had lemonade and dirt cake at whose house this week. Who took their kids to the open skate at the arena, and whose hip replacement was working out real well.

If I didn't finish my work Friday, I would come back in Saturday morning. Some Saturdays I came back in even when I had finished, just for fun. I liked to watch the week's edition come together on the office's big snazzy desktop. My boss Britta fit everything together like a puzzle, both logical and attractive. The front-page headlines and the church schedule. The recipes for wild mushroom soup and rhubarb cake in *Chef's Corner*. My favorite column, *In Our Past*—photographs of the stark winter logging camps and Pioneer Picnics from twenty and fifty and a hundred years ago. The crime report, the arena schedule, the bowling scores, the Senior Citizen lunch menus—for each item its own perfect spot.

Often Britta let me edit a photo or an article, or asked me to call to check the spelling of someone's name. She asked for my input on the layout, too.

Britta paid me $13 an hour. It was generous, certainly more than any other kid in town made and probably more than most of the adults. Britta's rich parents lived in a ritzy suburb of Minneapolis and were funding her small-town newspaper adventure.

It usually came to about fifty bucks a week. I had about $350 saved at Aspen Bank. Aside from gas and my fancy shampoo, most weeks I used at least some of my check to cover a few groceries as well.

Plus cat food and litter. Enid had been my idea. She kept the place from feeling too lonely when Tonya wasn't there.

Two hundred dollars a month wasn't enough to live on. But how many times had Britta said I had a future in journalism? And she had made even clearer hints than that. I was almost certain that if she had her way, I would come on full-time as assistant editor after I graduated from high school in the spring.

"Wow, June," she had said—how many times? Too many to count!—"great work. Sometimes I think you're ready to do my job."

I picked up the small notebook I kept on my nightstand so I could write out some numbers. As I did, I glanced at the stack of paper next to my notebook: college application forms.

Zee had printed these at the computer lab at school. She was smart. She knew I was not like her, constantly on Twitter or a news comments section yelling at people about their ignorant bigotry or their atrocious grammar. She knew I'd be more likely to fill out an application if I were allowed to use my favorite blue pen. Especially if the task were accompanied by a trip to the bakery and a cup of coffee that was actually mostly chocolate.

When I got all of my information penned down like a medieval scribe, Zee said, she would fill out the online forms for me herself.

Zee had already been accepted at Macalester College in St. Paul. As she never failed to remind me, I had missed the major deadlines for early admission everywhere. There were still a few Twin Cities schools where I could get an app in by the end of January for regular admission. It was more competitive now. But my grades and test scores, while not quite as high as Zee's, were good.

I'd printed my full name, June Aster Bergeron, onto the form. Also my address and social security number. Everything else was still blank.

It was soothing to do some neat multiplication problems. And *voilà*—full-time at the *North Star* at $13 an hour would cover the $325 a month for the apartment and the $80 for utilities. My phone, groceries. A few extras.

On the Saturday sessions at the newspaper office, Britta was training me in for the job. We both knew it. She had needed someone for six months now, ever since her last assistant editor had gone to work for a paper in a bigger town.

Britta didn't want to look for anyone else. I was sure of it. She had been working overtime all year, biding her time until I graduated.

Though she hadn't yet formally asked me. And I hadn't given her a clear indication of whether my answer would be yes or no.

Would she let me start now if I asked her? Without a high school diploma?

Of course, if she did let me—that would mean I'd have to quit school.

For the first time that night, I cried, just a little. But it wasn't about my mother. School wasn't perfect. But I had enjoyed certain aspects of it for a couple of years now.

When I was very young, I hadn't liked it at all. For a long time, I had been at Tonya's mercy when it came to how I dressed and whether or not my lunch bill was paid on time.

But that had changed as I got older. Particularly this year. The other kids were getting more mature and focused on their futures. I couldn't remember the last time any of the boys had drawn a picture of a cow with my name on it, or called Zee a dyke and shoved her into the boys' locker room.

The school was the center of everything in Aulneau; the whole town revolved around it. When you were a senior, that meant the whole town revolved around *you*.

I loved it. Loved how everyone in town knew not only how the volleyball and football teams were doing, but which play we were putting up, the Student Council votes, the prom theme. If I went into the Ben Franklin or the Holiday or the hairdresser's, it was important to whoever was asking if I had placed at the speech meet in Charlette on Saturday. How Zee's solo for contests was coming along.

For me, there was always a special pride and sympathy. I could tell that because of Tonya being who she was, and my lack of even the ghost of a father, people thought it was really something that I had turned into such a good kid. I'd felt cared for and admired—since I was in 10th grade, practically a celebrity—by all the adults in town.

Well—almost all of them.

I wiped tears from my cheek with my scarf. I hadn't bothered to take it off yet. I still had my stocking hat on, too.

Then I looked across the room. Tonya's bed was pushed up against the south window to get the most light. Her windowsill was lined with pots: thyme, oregano, chamomile, lemon balm.

Behind the plants, whatever parts of the window were not banked up with small drifts of new snow were covered with feathery curls of thick frost. Outside, snow was still falling, though lightly now.

After a minute, I stood up and went to the sink, filled the plastic pitcher we kept there, and went to Tonya's bed. I watered each plant slowly, careful not to overdo it and spill dirty water on the comforter.

I put the pitcher down carefully on her rickety wooden nightstand. Her incense burner held a little burnt cone. I crushed it, then touched her pillow, leaving a few grains of ash.

"Mom," I said aloud, though softly.

What did I expect—for her to materialize? Wearing a yellow fairy dress, with a beatific smile and flowers in her hair?

Well. Maybe.

Wasn't that the least she could do?

Of course, if I *really* wanted her to come . . .

"Tonya," I said.

What would I have asked her, had her ghost actually arrived?

What had happened, of course. Why she had blown herself away.

Maybe even other questions first. Like who my father was. What hope did I have of ever finding that out now?

Would she be any more willing to discuss that question now that she was dead than she had been when she was alive?

When I was very little and had begun to ask, Tonya would make up cute stories. My father lived in the stars and slid down to Earth on the northern lights. He was a timber wolf who could turn into a man.

The first time—I was nine—I had frowned and said, "No, but really—who was he?" had marked a milestone in the parent-child relationship, what there was of it, I had with Tonya.

She had frowned, too. And after that, no more stories.

She also started leaving me alone without a babysitter. Old enough to ask serious questions, old enough to boil my own spaghetti and to remember to lock the door before I went to bed at night.

The only other word she ever gave me on the subject came when, the terrible thought having suddenly occurred to me when I was about thirteen, I asked her in horror, "It's not Frank, is it?"

Tonya said no. She was laughing so hard at the idea, I figured I could believe her.

If Tonya did appear after death in a long, filmy dress, I imagined, her hair would also be all gray now. Or even sparkling white.

Yes. In life, while Tonya's hair was mostly still dark brown, it had started to get a fair amount of gray in it. While Frank was always trying to get her to dye it—"Don't you think your mom would look good as a blond, Juney?"—she wouldn't. She wanted to be natural. This was what happened when you were thirty-nine, she said. This is what she would look like at thirty-nine.

I loved it. I was born when Tonya was only twenty-one, and my whole life she had always looked young. The gray hairs made her look like more of a mother.

Over the past year, Tonya and I had started to have real, scream-it-out fights over the father question.

Or—did it count as a fight when only one of the participants was shouting so hard that she drooled and had to re-apply her thick veneer of Black Orchid lipstick? While the other simply moved quietly around the apartment in a flannel shirt and fuzzy pigtails, her hands clasped, her eyes half-closed, like a hippie monk under a vow of silence?

Enid meowed. I had been standing for several minutes with the water pitcher in my hand, just staring at the frosty window behind Tonya's bed.

I rinsed out Enid's dish and gave her some fresh water, too.

I looked at the clock on Tonya's nightstand. 11:30. The glowing digital numbers reminded me of my phone. It had gone dead at the police station after more than two hours of searching for service in the woods.

I went to my coat and pulled my phone out of the pocket. When I plugged it in, it immediately started to light up with voicemails and texts. Jack must have called everyone.

From Uncle Aaron, a simple *On my way.* It was a six-hour drive from Minneapolis, so he wouldn't be here until the morning.

I looked at the one from Britta: *J what happened? Call me as soon as you get this.*

I stared at it for a while. Yes. I had decided. I texted Britta back.

I'd take the job immediately, if she'd have me. I'd ask her tonight and get things settled as soon as possible.

Quitting school would be awful. Zee would kill me. We wouldn't get to go to any more Knowledge Bowl meets together, or finish our final performance project on *Hamlet,* or craft our clever and cutting final words for the yearbook.

But it was the responsible thing to do. And better than being a beggar or a whore.

"Are you kidding me, Juney?" said Tonya's ghost that wasn't there. "Why do you have to be so serious all the time? You're a kid. This is a time to have fun."

"Then you shouldn't have done this to me," I said to the empty room.

SIX

I heard a car drive up; Zee's brakes squeaked faintly. Her family lived on the west side of town, just on the other side of the bay.

I went to the window and watched as Jack and Zee got out of their cars and spoke briefly. I couldn't hear what they said. They stood far apart on the street, both with their arms crossed. Then Jack got back into his car and left.

I wondered for the first time if the two of them would have been friends, if I hadn't been in the picture. All this time, had I been the glue that stuck them unwillingly together?

Footsteps thundered up the stairs. Zee knocked on the apartment door and I unlocked and opened it. The lock on the street-level door had been broken for years.

Zee barely looked at me before pulling me into a hug.

"Hey," she said.

I shook my head into her bomber jacket and kept my face buried there a while. Her coat smelled of cigarette smoke. I didn't mention it as she pulled it off and sat down in the rocking chair near the door. I sat back down on my bed.

"Tell me what happened." Zee leaned forward, her elbows on her knees, her face in her hands.

"Or tell me what I can do," she added quickly, sitting up straight again.

I gave her what I think was my first smile of the night. I was so glad Zee was here, my favorite person in the world.

"Could you make me a cup of tea?" I said.

Zee sprang from her chair and it banged against the wall. She steadied it before busying herself at the stove while I curled up against the wall with a pillow and Enid and watched her.

Zee, graceful Zee, her body as tall and boyish as mine was tall and grown-womanish.

I had looked this way, with big boobs and hips, since we were about thirteen. That year, I'd looked in the mirror and done a frank assessment. I had two choices: try to hide my shape with baggy jeans and men's shirts and look like a giant lumber-jack version of my mother, or decide that my dramatic curves looked nice and play them up. Making the choice to go with the latter was unnerving at first. Then it was pretty fun.

That same year, Zee had begun to look at my rapidly devel-oping chest with a horror she couldn't quite hide. A fear that the same fate might be ahead for her.

It wasn't. These days, she strutted her slender, muscular body around with an almost cocky satisfaction.

It was partly a show. Overcompensation. School in Aulneau hadn't ever been easy for Zee.

I suspected she believed she had made her body look this way entirely by the sheer force of her own volition. She did lift weights every day after school to build up the muscles in her arms and legs. She also sometimes flattened what boobs she did have with Ace bandages. But basically, she was just built like her willowy mother.

She would have liked to be two inches taller. Five-eleven would have been perfect.

Zee kept her straight sandy hair cut short. Today she wore a man's soft white t-shirt with jeans worn low enough to show the waistband of her boxer shorts. She'd used a blow dryer and wax to sculpt her hair into a spiky James Dean quiff. On other days, she went for a more severe slickback, Draco-style.

I kept my own hair in a sleek flapper bob. I had been dyeing my hair, naturally the same ash brown as my mother's, a black-ish auburn since I was fourteen. I always applied plenty of shine spray for a nice dramatic effect.

Enough, as Tonya liked to say, "to seal a wood floor." Zee's dad poked fun at her in the same way. He ran a garage and liked to offer his automotive spray for her styling routine, a joke he thought endlessly funny.

Zee and I were so alike, it was no wonder we were best friends.

She brought me my tea in a dainty flowered cup on a saucer, just the way I liked it.

"I did chamomile," she said. "I figured you'd want to get some sleep tonight."

"That's great. Thank you." It felt good to cradle the warm cup in my hands. I looked at Zee across the room rocking in the rickety chair. The old wooden joints creaked; Zee tapped her damp sneaker on the floor; and, looking fretful, ran her hand back over her James Dean hair.

I relaxed a little. In the mellow lamplight, this looked like a scene I could recognize and enjoy. One I was watching, or act-ing, rather than living through.

For a moment, I pretended Zee and I were two characters in a play. I had all the details on the latest sordid crime to happen in our trendy seaside town, and Zee was dying to hear them. The crime didn't affect me personally, of course; other than that, luckily enough, I had been on the spot to witness it. The bloody body that had come crashing down through the ceil-ing during a posh event. The art museum that had its windows smashed while I was gazing at a gleaming Van Gogh.

Zee, in a vest and a jaunty scarf tied around her neck, was my partner at our detective agency. Or she was an old friend from our college days, now an artist living in a scruffy but styl-ish flat in the poor part of town. She scandalized and yet also fascinated and attracted everyone who saw her. With her short hair speckled with paint and her knees in manly tweed trousers thrown apart and the way she gave cool and cagey answers to the police when they came to demand she tell everything she knew about the counterfeit bills being manufactured in the seedy building across the street or the body in the library.

My office in this fantasy was on the seashore. The day was sunny. A breeze passed through frothy blue curtains. I could almost hear music spilling out of boardwalk cafés, gulls crying as they banked over the glittering water. The smells of sea salt and sweet fried food drifting in . . .

The illusion dissolved quickly. Light from the lamp in the apartment was mellow only because its plastic shade was dingy with a layer of dust I couldn't scrub off.

Zee and I stared at one another for a while.

"I haven't cried," I said finally. "Do you think that's weird?"

Zee shook her head. "You're not a crier."

Actually, I cried easily, even luxuriously, over things like *Romeo and Juliet* and the death of Snape. Over difficult assignments at school and cute pictures of Zee and me as children.

But I knew what Zee meant. My fundamental griefs involving Tonya I had worked to harden myself to long ago.

"This doesn't feel like sadness. I don't know what this feels like."

I told Zee everything, including Frank's suspicious behavior. At the end, Zee's forehead crinkled.

She was silent for a while. Then she said, "I'm so sorry, June."

I waited for more. That was it. She hadn't reacted exactly as I'd expected.

What had I expected? Shock and surprise. Well. Maybe Jack had given her some of the details already?

"It's strange, isn't it?" I said.

Zee nodded slowly. "Yeah. For sure." She was studying a point on the wall, past my head.

"Frank. I think he's hiding something."

53

"Right. Well. He might be."

"Drugs, maybe. Don't you think?"

Slowly, Zee focused back on me. "You mean, she was on something when she—" She closed her mouth abruptly.

"Or she owed somebody money? Zee"—I looked at her closely—"did Frank or Tonya ever try to sell you drugs? Or ask you to sell them?"

"Ask *me*?" Zee's eyes widened. She flicked them on me for a second. Then she looked away again. "People don't kill themselves because they're high on pot, June," she muttered.

"That's not what I meant. But maybe," I mused, "that *was* it. Maybe she was on something stronger?"

"I wouldn't know about that."

I watched her. I felt a familiar faint prickle in my left armpit. Sometimes I developed a hideous stress rash when I was overwhelmed at school or worried about something.

Zee hadn't answered my question, so I asked it again.

"No," she said finally.

"Are you lying to me?"

Zee narrowed her eyes. "I don't lie to you."

"You keep things from me."

Such as: one awkward day this past summer, Frank had come up to me on the sidewalk in front of the newspaper office, smirking around a cigarette. Telling me he and Tonya had run into my girlfriend, or boyfriend, or whatever it was, at a house party in Pluie, the closest town across the international border.

"You didn't tell me you were boozing it up with my mother. I had to hear it from *Frank*," I said to Zee now.

"I wasn't. I told you. I left as soon as they got there. God knows what they were doing at a high-school party."

"Well"—my resentment dissipated for a moment as I started to think—"maybe they were trying to find some kids to sell drugs for them at school?"

"Which kids?"

"Whoever they could get to do it."

Zee said in a prissy voice, "'*Whom*ever.'"

I rolled my eyes and she choked out a sulky apology. Her tone was still snappish when she said, "Well. I don't know. If they were trying to recruit drug dealers, I don't know anything about it." I looked at her and she looked back at me.

"Why are you yelling at me?" I said.

Zee sighed and put her hands over her face. She sank back into the rocking chair. "I'm not. I'm sorry, June. I'm just thinking, I guess, well, if it *is* something like that—that sounds dangerous. So let the police handle it."

"Maybe they won't think of it. So maybe I should tell Jack about the party . . . "

"Sure. Go ahead. But then just—focus on other things, okay?"

Zee still wouldn't look at me.

I said soothingly, "Sure. Okay," and started talking about something else—Uncle Aaron's impending arrival—until Zee's brown eyes peered out at me from between her long, pale fingers again.

My armpit started to really itch. I resisted an urge to scratch. I finished my tea and Zee got up to make me another cup.

As she ran the water, she was frowning faintly. I knew that expression well. It was similar to the one she used to get when we first met at age six. She looked that way whenever teachers, kids, and even her own parents called her by name: "Sue" or "Suzanne." Or, worst of all, "Suzie."

Something was wrong, my new friend's expression said. Something was wrong, even though even she couldn't say quite what.

Though "Suzie" was where I had come up with the name she still went by today. As soon as I pronounced it, Zee had beamed. I was throwing her a big red rubber kickball on the playground at the time. She was so surprised and happy, she dropped it.

I was proud of that. Now that we were growing up, I was beginning to feel that coming up with that name might turn out to be one of the best and most important things I'd ever do in my life.

In kindergarten, Zee and I had looked a lot alike. Because Tonya always dressed me in miniature wife-beaters and boys' overalls, and shaved my head to make my hair easier to take care of. Once I began to bring my new friend home to play, Zee even shared my early childhood trait of being covered with inexpert henna tattoos. Tonya practiced them on us before she did them on herself.

As we got older, I began to pick out my own clothes. For birthday and Christmas presents, I asked my Aunt Sylvi in Minneapolis for frilly dresses that I found online.

It made Zee sad. I could tell. When we first met, Zee had probably thought she'd found another human like her. Another girl who, when stuffed into a pink skirt or shiny shoes, wanted to writhe like a snake in the dust until she shook them off.

And her mother was trying to make her grow out her hair. Zee would come over to my house and beg Tonya to cut it. Tonya always did it, no matter how many furious emails she got from Zee's mother. Tonya thought that Zee should be who she wanted to be.

I felt I was doing that, too. I liked the attention I got when I carefully put together one of my smart, old-fashioned out-fits. Dirndl dresses and boat-neck collars. Suit-coat tops and neck bows. I liked it when Ms. Karbo, our favorite teacher, said, "That dress is flattering on you, June."

Ms. Karbo, the only teacher of color in the school, had been Zee's top choice as faculty advisor for her Diversity Club when she started it in the ninth grade. There were no queer teachers to choose from. Her suggestion that we come up with a list of events threw Zee for a loop.

"I thought it would be more, like—we get together and talk about what it's like to be different," she said.

Then Ms. Karbo had sent us out recruiting. The range of reactions ran from tepid interest to hostility.

"A diversity club?" Carla Vincent had looked back and forth between us and smiled faintly at, I can only assume, our pallid complexions. "You guys?" She looked wistful when she found out Ms. Karbo would be serving her family's recipes for fry bread and squash soup at our potluck for Indigenous Peoples Day. Carla was one of only three Ojibwe kids at our school.

"It's *me*," Zee had wailed to Ms. Karbo, cross-legged on her classroom floor, her face buried in her arms. "No one wants to be associated with *me*."

"I do!" I bent down as best as I could in my polka-dot kitten heels.

In the apartment, I watched Zee pour the steaming water for my tea. As of today, she and I were still the only two members of her club.

But still she had changed a lot in the last three years, from that timid girl weeping on the floor.

She looked up when we heard a knock. Then my name spoken in a soft voice. I only just barely recognized it as Britta's, who rarely did anything quietly.

I told her to come in and stood up. Britta opened the door and peered uncertainly into the room. Then she came forward and put her hands on my arms, as high as she could reach. She was like a slim little Swedish elf with very blond hair.

Her ice-blue eyes were rimmed with red. She gripped me fiercely.

"June. I can't believe it," she said.

I nodded. I didn't trust myself to speak just then. Seeing Britta so upset was unsettling. It was almost worse than watching Frank kneel by Tonya in the snow. Britta didn't have the illusions about Tonya that Frank did. But still she liked her a lot. Liked her winsome, whacky nature and the excursions they went on together. The two of them would lug a canoe on their scrawny shoulders for two or three miles through the woods.

I was never sure if Tonya whole-heartedly returned the feeling. For her, the friendship might have been more transactional. Britta often paid Tonya to be a guide when Britta's parents and friends drove up from the Twin Cities thirsty for wild adventures, their SUVs stuffed with thousands of dollars of gear.

Britta was smart and brassy and funny. I liked her, even though I was often the butt of her jokes.

"Britta," I blurted out, "I need to talk to you. About the paper."

I felt Zee give us a sharp sidelong look. Too late, I realized I should have waited to bring up the job with Britta until a moment when Zee wasn't around.

Britta looked confused. "Okay."

"Please sit down," I said meekly.

I returned to my seat on my own bed and Britta sat on Tonya's. There wasn't room in our place for a couch. Britta's long, white-blond hair was pulled into two pigtails that hung on either side of her rosy baby face. She was wearing striped overalls. At twenty-six, she could have been mistaken for one of our classmates at school. Looking childish and sweet definitely helped Britta get away with things.

Zee stood with her back against the counter and crossed her arms, looking back and forth between Britta and me. My fresh cup of tea sat cooling beside her. I glanced at it longingly.

"Okay, June. What about the paper?"

"Oh." All of the sudden I lost my nerve. "Never mind. We can talk about it later. Jack called you?"

Britta nodded. "He didn't tell me much. What happened?"

I told the story from the beginning again. As Britta listened carefully, nodding and often stopping me to ask questions, I saw her change. It wasn't that she was no longer sympathetic. But I could see the wheels turning, too. It gave me a stirring feeling that was neither good nor bad.

When I was done, she said, "A gun? That doesn't sound like Tonya."

"That's what I said!"

"Hmm." Britta leaned back against the wall, her short legs stuck out straight on the bed. She looked up at the ceiling and softly clucked her tongue.

"Britta, what do you think about Frank?"

"You said Frank mentioned Duluth?"

I thought about it. "No. I was the one who brought up Duluth. Those missing women, you know?"

"The ones who were killed?" Zee said.

"Yes," I said slowly. "Three of them. The other two I don't think they've found.

"Wait," I added after a moment, looking at Britta. "You don't think—"

Britta sat up straight, her hands on her hips. "I don't think anything," she said sharply. "I'm just asking questions."

I stared at her. "I got the feeling that Frank didn't want to talk about Duluth. That he was changing the subject."

"Okay. And can you tell me again about the note?"

"Britta, look behind you on the shelf. You see the row of notebooks there? Those are Tonya's." I asked her to pull one out.

"Just flip through . . . What do you notice?" Before Britta had even gone through one of them, I asked her to pull out another. "All in pencil. Right?"

"June, I'm inclined to follow Jack's thinking on that one. Listen," Britta said, when I protested, "I know about Tonya's pen thing. But I don't think it was as absolute as you're remembering. See?" She held up a page in one of the notebooks. Most of it was written in red ink. A few words were scratched out.

"That's red, though," I said after a second. "She liked red."

When neither Britta nor Zee spoke, I looked down at my hands. "She wanted to be able to erase everything. Say goodbye and pretend something had never existed."

"Yes. But—"

"It goes back to pencil at the bottom of the page."

"Be careful, June. It's easy, when you don't want to believe something, to see signs and hidden messages that lead you to the conclusion you'd rather find."

"I'm not doing that. Tonya was the one who always did that. I just want to know the truth."

"What truth?" Both Britta and I looked at Zee. Her tone was rather harsh. She was leaning back in the rocking chair again, her arms crossed, her feet planted to keep the chair from rocking. My lovely chamomile long forgotten.

"Why she did what she did." Then, without looking at her, "Or, if maybe someone else could have—"

"You said the gun was in her hand." Zee spoke more gently this time.

"Sometimes a scene is staged . . ."

"Only on TV . . ."

"The police will be able to tell that, won't they?" I asked Britta.

"Yes. They'll be looking at all that. Well, they'd better look at it, anyway . . . If not, they'll be hearing from me . . . But about the note. Like I said, I'm not convinced about the pen thing. The signature, on the other hand . . ." Britta stopped and stared off into the air as if she were seeing "Tonya Elizabeth Bergeron" scripted there in smoke.

I said, "She never wrote her name that way unless she felt like she had to. For something official."

"Unless she had to," Britta repeated thoughtfully. "You're right. What does this signature—her full signature—do? It makes this note official. Binding. It's Tonya. She wrote it. Yes.

It's her without a doubt. No one can dispute it. No one can say, well, this is just a scribble, she might have written it, she might not have . . .

"But, at the same time," she went on, "does it make it *hers*? A piece of writing written on her own terms? Wouldn't that have been important to her?"

"Yes." I glanced at Zee, sitting stone-faced in her chair. "I think it would have. She didn't even like her full name. She was named after both her grandmothers. She didn't like that. She wanted her own name. To be her own person. Original."

"Maybe that's why she liked that crazy signature of hers?" Britta said.

"So you think that maybe—she *was* trying to send us a message?"

"Well. I don't know. It surprises me, is all."

We all sat quietly for a few minutes. I ran my fingers softly over my itchy skin without thinking about it. I caught myself and bit my thumbnail instead.

It didn't work to distract me, so I got up and grabbed one of the journals off of Tonya's bed and took it back to mine. Leafing through it, I stopped on a random page to briefly read one of the entries. It sounded like the transcription of a dream. Tonya was living in a commune in the woods with what sounded like a bunch of other hippies. Starlight and Gray Feather and Howls-at-the-Moon, whose specialty in the group was making a disgusting-sounding soap out of bear fat. Tonya lived in a tree. She was building a rope bridge to Starlight's tree.

I turned the page to see if I showed up in this scene anywhere. But the entry ended after only a few more lines. When I saw how it was signed—in red ink, and with Tonya's full signature—I closed the book softly and placed it behind me on the bed.

Britta said, "June, do you want me to stay here tonight?"

My eyes met Zee's. "Well—of course you can if you want to. But I think Zee's staying with me. Right?"

"Of course I am."

Britta nodded and slid forward on Tonya's bed until her elfin feet were on the floor. "Okay. Well, can you think of anything you need? I might head over to the office."

"You're going to work tonight?"

"I have a few things I want to check on . . ."

"About this?"

Britta nodded, biting her lip. Zee made a disgruntled sound in her throat.

"All right, well—Britta." I had to do it. Even in front of Zee. There was no where I could ask her to go so that Britta and I could speak in private. I wouldn't be able to sleep if I didn't get this settled before I went to bed.

I spoke in a rush. I said quite firmly that I had made the decision to quit school and come to work full-time for Britta on the paper as her assistant editor. Immediately.

Of course, I added timidly, I might want to go to school for a day or two, maybe a week, if that was all right—speak to my teachers—maybe even sit in on a couple of classes, just to say goodbye—

Tears came to my eyes. I didn't let them fall.

Britta laughed. It wasn't a long and sustained, tear-filled belly-breaker or anything like that—but a laugh it was indeed. A short, sharp bark of a laugh that made me feel as if she'd tripped me on the playground just for the joy of watching me fall.

"June—you can't be serious," she said.

Looking at my face, she must have quickly recognized her mistake. Usually, the mistake was mine. And usually, my redneck gaffes did send Britta practically rolling on the floor. Like the time she told me to find a place in the paper for a press release sent by a big tobacco company. Miracle of miracles, it described a new study that had found that cigarettes didn't cause cancer after all. Thinking of Zee, I completed the task zealously and with an enormous sense of relief. Or there was the day we were paging through old newspapers hunting for details for *In Our Past*. Britta pointed to a photo from the high-school play and made the innocent-sounding remark that Aulneau had certainly had many more Black people in the past than it did now. When I agreed in surprise, Britta hooted and squealed. But how was I supposed to know what blackface looked like, having never seen it before?

Tonight, Britta rushed forward and tried to hold me again. I turned away stiffly and closed my eyes.

"Oh, June, I'm sorry . . . I didn't mean to laugh . . . I've got such a big mouth! It's not that—listen. You are great. You are so great. But you know that I need someone who—"

I still had my eyes squeezed shut. Britta tried a different tack.

"June, you're not quitting school," she said desperately. "You're just about to graduate."

"I don't know what I'm going to live on, though. I don't know how I'll pay for anything."

"You'll stay with me," Zee said. I looked at her and she said softly, "It *is* crazy, June."

"It's the right thing to do." I lifted my chin.

"Right for whom?" Zee said.

"And your uncle will help you," said Britta. "He's not going to—"

"Uncle Aaron doesn't have anything. He's already helping Aunt Sylvi and Uncle Rich."

"June, I'm sure your mother had *something* put away—"

"Is that a joke?" I turned and glared at Britta.

Now it was her turn to lower her eyes. Zee and I exchanged a grim look.

"Okay," Britta said carefully, after a moment.

"So you don't want me? You don't want me to be your assistant?"

"Maybe someday! But June—you don't have the experience yet. You need to study. Get a degree."

"I thought I was studying with you. Like, an apprenticeship kind of thing." I closed my eyes again and covered my face with my hands. I could feel my skin burning. I wanted to run and hide, or, even better, stomp the creaky floor until it splintered, tumble completely out of sight.

"June, I'm sorry—"

"No. Never mind. I get it." I got it, all right; Britta had never wanted me to stay here, any more than my mother had.

I didn't say it. It would have been childish. Demeaning. I felt a strange swell of revulsion that turned my stomach. I kept my face hidden and shuddered.

"June, please don't worry. We're going to take care of you. We all love you so much. The whole town. You know very well everyone will pitch in. All I have to do is put the word out, and—"

"No. Don't you dare."

The rash bloomed out over my chest with an unpleasant heat. I couldn't help it. I scratched.

SEVEN

woke early the next morning. The sky outside was still a very dark gray. When I first opened my eyes, my mind tricked me.

As usual, I looked across the room at Tonya's bed to see if she were there.

On normal days, if her bed were empty, my mind would turn to recalling the night before. Had Tonya told me that she might be out all night? Had she said where she was going?

If she had, I might start musing on the places or people she had mentioned. The pool tables at Tamarack. The campground at Namekaa Point. Brenda Fish, who lived just north of Landby.

Or people and places Tonya had described more vaguely—someone she had gone to school with, who had moved away in the eighth grade. They were going out for a drink to catch up. A house party southwest of here. Where? Makwa? Oh, farther than that . . . almost to Fever River . . .

Or—and this was more likely—if Tonya hadn't told me anything about where she was going, or even that she was going at all, I just looked at her empty bed for a few minutes. I'd try to remember what she had been wearing the day before.

In case I had to call in a description.

Of course, sometimes she *was* there. In the winter, her slight frame huddled under an enormous pile of quilts. It was cold there against the window.

I'd look at her dark head for a few minutes. Sometimes I got up and quietly tied on an apron and made for the kitchen, a few miniature appliances and a strip of green linoleum in the corner near the door. I'd make coffee and fry her some eggs. If the smell didn't wake her, I'd eat them myself and wait. Eventually Tonya would stir and make a few soft noises in her sleep. She'd stretch a little. She'd sit up and give me a smile that had a little pain in it—sometimes some genuine physical pain from a hangover. But also she looked tiny and shy, like a child. And slightly ashamed, wearing a rumpled nightshirt or her jeans from the night before. Looking at her giantess of a daughter, otherwise known as Betty Crocker, looming by the dinky ancient stove with her blue-and-white checked apron still on.

"Well, thanks, Juney," she'd say and yawn. Maybe just as an excuse to close her eyes. Or she'd look into her lap and use her fingers to comb through her long, tangled hair.

When I woke this particular morning, my mind granted me one extra moment of oblivion. I didn't remember what had happened the day before. I felt the usual mix of questions. Was Tonya here? If not, where?

No. There was a blond head in Tonya's bed. Zee.

Yes . . .

And someone was on the floor in a sleeping bag. Uncle Aaron. He had managed to creep in without waking me up.

Seeing them was a concrete reminder that what I was beginning to remember was true. My usual morning feeling did not apply anymore.

Would, in fact, never apply again.

The usual worry didn't go away. Instead, it began to swell. Rapidly, like one of those colored capsules that with a drop of water balloons into a sponge.

It was pushing aside everything good and comfortable. Laying every raw part of me open and bare to a horror worse than any I had felt on any previous morning when I had wondered where my mother was, who she was with, was she safe, was she lost, had she been in a car accident. Was she lying dead in a ditch somewhere.

I could barely remember the last time I'd felt as if Tonya were the parent and I were the child. Our relationship had always been more like a chase. Me chasing after her and trying to get her to stay with me where it was safe. But then, even when I had her, not being able to get out of her what I wanted.

If I had only held on a little more tightly, screamed at her a little louder!

Now she was dead. I had failed. The worst had happened.

And where was she now?

I started to understand why some people spent their lives paying attention to that question. Going to church and talking about heaven and all that.

Not me. No. Perhaps I had thought of the grandma and grandpa I'd never known smiling down on me from some vague sunny place . . .

But those nebulous thoughts and images didn't feel like enough to deal with—*this*.

What was my mother now? An angel? A ghost?

Or was she just—a *thing*? A body? The body I had seen frozen in the woods?

Tonya would have told me absolutely not. She was a great believer in ghosts.

In general, whatever she believed in, I believed in the opposite. But I didn't like that thought very well right now.

Nothingness. It was an awful, bleak possibility.

When I really could have used something nicer—something full of warmth and color.

What if she was just gone? Done? Nothing? Would she never feel the sun on her face again? Here or anywhere?

While I—I *would*. While I was feeling something now. Was in the world now. While she was—simply—*not*.

All of the sudden I was overwhelmed by these gaping thoughts. I was desperately afraid. That I would never feel happy—or even just all right—again.

Lying in bed, I gripped my blankets in my fists. Everything was terrible in the world. The sick feeling in my stomach. The prickly rash that made me feel as if I were being stabbed by the fiery proboscises of a thousand mosquitoes at once. I pulled the sleeve of my pajamas down off my shoulder and looked at the infectious-looking wash of purple-red dots and streaks spreading down my chest.

The gray light in the room. The fact that while Zee and Uncle Aaron were just yards away, I felt completely alone.

My throat and chest felt raw and cold, as if I had been running. I wanted to cry. What a relief it would be to cry!

But even the possibility of ever being able to cry again felt far away. I felt that this relief might never be available to me again.

Slowly I thought of something. I stared out the window. I told myself I could stop thinking. Gave myself permission to do so. I didn't have to do or think anything until I saw the first faint blush of pink in the morning sky.

And when I did see it, I told myself, I *still* wouldn't have to think. No. Not quite yet. Instead, I would just move. I'd reach over onto my nightstand and check my phone. Just that.

When I did, I saw I had a message from Britta.

It said, *Found something. Meet me at the office when you get up.*

EIGHT

I n order to not wake up Uncle Aaron and Zee, I didn't make coffee or even open the refrigerator.

As soon as I swung my legs quietly over the side of the bed, Enid started to meow. I poured her dry food into my hand before placing it carefully in her metal dish.

I rubbed aloe gel into my inflamed skin. The hives were now beginning to travel up onto my neck. The gel felt nice and cool for about thirty seconds. After that, it was only sticky.

I pulled on long underwear and pants and a heavy collared shirt and a sweater, laced up my boots over two pairs of socks, then piled on a scarf and hat and two pairs of mittens. I did not like to be cold. It took forever, when I had to do everything so quietly.

I had the vague idea that I might stop at the grocery store or the bakery after I'd crossed the bridge into the main part of town. I'd pick up coffee and a roll or a hard-boiled egg and some sesame sticks.

But I didn't. What was it going to be like, the first time I walked into a store?

Had word gotten around? Did people know by now what had happened? How were they going to act?

And how would *I* act? Would I do something crazy and un-expected—like swear, or laugh wildly, or push over a display, or throw my arms around an old woman? It seemed to me that anything was possible. What did death do to you?

Or, if word hadn't gotten around, I could imagine someone saying, "Jeez, June, you'd better get going. You're going to be late for school."

Yes. Because it was a school day—Monday. One of the yellow buses passed me on the bridge, leaving behind a cloud of white-gray smoke. I didn't look to see who was in it. Most kids my age drove to school, anyway.

I glanced over the guardrail down at the frozen bay. A bird was hopping around in the gray-blue shadows under the bridge. It shook its wings. I wondered what it thought it was going to find down there.

It was a surprise to find that the town was still the same as it had been yesterday. The flat landscape, the main street wide enough for a row of angle-parked cars on each side. The businesses housed in mostly low and unornamented buildings made of aluminum.

Walking through the six or seven inches of new snow on the sidewalk felt almost good. The first good thing that morning.

One foot after the other. I got tired. It was nice to have something to work at. I got a little sweaty, even, and pulled off my outer pair of mittens.

When I got to the door of the *North Star Herald* on Central, I wanted to keep going. Walk for several miles. I wished the street went on forever.

Then I saw someone up ahead of me on the sidewalk. A man just about to go into the hardware store. I squinted—it was Frank.

He saw me. A second later, he waved. I ducked into the *Herald* and firmly shut the door.

"I'm here," I said.

The newspaper office: a bright and pleasant place. Framed copies of old papers and concert posters on the white walls. A few pieces of dark red furniture scattered around the room: wheeled chairs, a futon with a black frame, a tall metal garbage can with shiny paint like nail polish. Britta was alone in there. She was the only person, other than me, who worked on the paper.

The office wasn't always empty. People stopped in to pay subscriptions or talk about ads. The oldest people who wrote for the paper—most of the coffee columnists, the ancient retired librarian who did "The Reading Chair"—came to drop off handwritten copy, and once a week the museum archivist from the Tree Lake Historical Society brought in the tattered and yellowing photographs of dusty Fourth of July parades and the Hudson Bay post at Skunk Portage that we used for *In Our Past*.

I loved those pictures. A crowd on the deck of a steamboat in the bay. A woman with a team of mules, carrying a dainty parasol in one hand and holding up the top of her skirts over the mud and snow with the other. I liked it when someone in a picture was a member of my family—a Bergeron, a Ravndalen, a Mikenak. Sometimes he or she would be standing in a school class photo or a portrait of the Fair Board with someone from one of Jack's old clans: a Friesner or a Laverne.

Zee's family had moved to the area from Wisconsin when Zee was a baby. They were still newcomers here.

Once I pestered Britta into putting Uncle Aaron into *In Our Past's* "Twenty Years Ago" section: his second-place ribbon in the all-school pumpkin-growing contest. I clipped it out and sent it to him in Minneapolis. No news story Tonya had ever appeared in was anything I wanted her to be remembered for.

People also came into the office just to chat, or to complain about morning deliveries that were late or about the fact that Britta had printed this or that letter to the editor.

Often Britta was there from very early in the morning until the middle of the night. This morning, judging by the rumpled afghan on the futon and the fact that she was wearing the same overalls from the day before, it looked as if she'd never left the office last night at all.

Britta handled it all—she *was* the paper. She did the reporting and the writing of the major local articles, the photographs and the columnist payroll. She edited and proofread copy, including her own. She sold all the advertising and designed all the ads. She did the layout. The only job she sent out was the printing, which was done in Gabekana, a bigger town forty miles west. Every Wednesday, Britta got up at four a.m. to organize the kids who did the weekly town delivery, too.

At the end of my sophomore year, Britta had come to the journalism teacher Mr. Ogden to ask if he could recommend a student to write the "School News" column. The student who had been writing it for the last several years was graduating.

First, Mr. Ogden recommended Zee. She was the best writer in our grade. But Britta wanted someone who would also do some typing. This person would need to be able to decipher the spidery cursive of the coffee columnists, and luckily, there was no one who filled that description but me. I had taught myself to read and write cursive from an old handwriting workbook that I bought at the public library's sale one summer.

When I came into the office today, Britta was on the phone, saying, "Well, with my personal connection . . .."

When she saw me, she stood up and told whoever she was talking to she would call them back later.

"Hey, June. I'm glad you came," she said.

"Who was that?" I began to take off my coat and unwind my scarf.

"Just a friend of mine. Did you sleep okay? Have you eaten anything?"

"Yes."

I had slept, in fact—a strangely deep sleep. And I was not a big one for breakfast, anyway.

I stared Britta down for a second. She blinked her blue eyes innocently.

I had felt better the moment I stepped into the office—this

neat, cheerful, productive place. My gaping feeling had receded a little. And I suspected that once I sat in that chair next to Britta's and busied my mind . . .

I let the suspicious phone call go and sat down. Britta did, too. I picked up a pen off the desk, stuck the end of it in my mouth, and turned to look at the screen of the office computer, where an email was open.

"What did you find?" I said.

"Look at this, June." The email was from a friend of Britta's who wrote for the *Minneapolis Star Tribune*. This reporter was investigating connections between the women who had gone missing in the Duluth area. He said the number of cases went back even further than this past year.

"Is this the friend you were talking to?" I looked at Britta.

"No, someone else . . . Now, originally, these women and girls were from a lot of different places." Britta stood up and went to a regional map hanging on the wall behind her desk. She took a pin and stuck it into a spot just north of Ziibi. She pushed in several more in Minnesota, one in southern Manitoba, one in Winnipeg, two in North Dakota.

"A lot on those orange places . . . what are those?"

"You know, June. The reservations. Ishkode Lake. Érable."

I hadn't heard of Érable, but I did know the Ojibwe reservation at Ishkode Lake. For a period of time a few years ago, our sports teams and theirs had had a difficult time getting back and forth to our respective athletic matches, as their students and ours were forever slashing the other school's bus tires. The speech meets Zee and I went to there were less contentious.

I got up and looked closer at the pins. "And the connection to Duluth?"

Britta sighed and looked again at the map. "A lot of the women were last seen in Duluth and Superior. A lot of them were runaways, homeless, drug addicts. Why Duluth . . . Well. It's the port. There's a sex-trafficking ring based there."

I waited. "Okay."

"The stories are terrible."

"Like what?" I waited. "Tell me."

"Oh, June . . . like, their parents are addicts. They sell the girls for drug money."

"You're not serious," I said.

"Or a girl gets lured onto a boat at the dock. Some guy tells her there's drugs or food there. She's hungry. She's cold, she doesn't have anywhere to go. She's desperate. She's been abused at home, she's run away, her home was unstable, her parents were never around . . . Maybe the guy who gets her there has been pretending he's her boyfriend. She thinks he loves her. He's chosen this girl. Found someone who's disconnected from her family, her friends. Who disappears sometimes, who has a history of it." She paused. "Someone not a lot of people will notice is gone."

I said quietly, "And then what?"

"Well—then—these girls find out they have to have sex for this great food or drugs. Or they get drugged and wake up and they're out to sea."

"Out to *sea*?" I said. "Going where?"

"Thunder Bay. Sault Saint Marie. Somewhere to be sold. Or they're sold to the crew on the boat—"

"No. This kind of thing happens *here*? *Now*?"

"It happens everywhere," said Britta.

I was quiet for a minute as I looked at her.

"And you think—that this might have happened to Tonya," I said.

"Some things fit. But others don't—"

"Well," I said in a low voice, "except that they do." I hadn't reported her missing. Because she went missing all the time . . .

"June," Britta began to say.

"She didn't have a job. She didn't have any money. Maybe she was drinking in a bar in Duluth because she was feeling bad."

I closed my eyes, then quickly opened them again. In that split second of darkness, a nasty image had flashed into view.

Tonya lying in a dim room. Her naked body on a cold floor. And the floor was rocking a little. Gently. From the waves. She opened her eyes and wondered why she felt sick. It must be that rocking. Why was the room rocking? She must have the spins. But there was also a faintly fishy smell in the air. The lake. Yes. She had gone to a party on the lake. On a boat. So . . .

A man was sitting across from her in a chair. Watching her.

I had no idea how to imagine him. How old was he? What kind of clothes did devils wear?

Or two men. Three. She was surrounded.

Maybe even tied up. Her hands bound together. Her ankles. Is that how they did this?

Tonya, who hated to be stuck in one place. Trapped.

"Oh God, Britta . . ." I pressed my hands over my mouth.

"June, listen." Britta put a hand on my shoulder. "Now. Let's think this through. If something like this did happen—if Tonya went to Duluth four days ago and was kidnapped there, then how did she end up back here? And why?"

"She escaped," I said. "They took her. They raped her. She got away. But it was so terrible that then she—or they found her and they were afraid she would identify them, so they—"

"But why did she go to Duluth in the first place?"

"What does that matter?"

"It does matter, June. It doesn't make sense. Tonya had had her license revoked, remember? Why risk driving two hundred miles?"

I thought about it. For all Tonya's recklessness, she was usually careful about not driving when she'd lost her license temporarily. She hated going to jail. She asked me for rides. Or Britta. Frank.

I thought of Tonya bent over in the rocking chair a couple weeks before, hiding her face.

"Maybe something bad happened *before* she went to Duluth?" I said. "Something that made her feel like taking a risk?"

"Like what?"

"Losing the job at Otten's? Running out of money?"

"Maybe. But does going into despair over losing a job really fit with what we know about your mother?"

"Frank acted funny when I mentioned Duluth. Maybe he took her there."

"Hm. And lost track of her, somehow, when they were there together?"

"That could be it. Maybe Tonya was talking to some guy in a bar. Frank got jealous and left. But the guy turned out to be a trafficker."

"Well, but June—"

"Frank gets pissed and walks out and leaves her there alone. Then, later, he goes back to the place. But she's gone. She's not answering her phone. She won't call him back. He can't find her anywhere. When he came to the apartment, he was feeling guilty about something . . . something specific . . . I'm sure of it . . ."

"Maybe . . . "

"You said that a lot of women who are targeted and a lot of them who have gone missing are Native American. Right?"

"Yeah," Britta said sadly.

"Well. Tonya had dark hair. And her skin was tanner than mine." I thrust my own pale hand out for her to see.

Britta narrowed her eyes. "June—"

Plus, I continued, Tonya certainly *thought* she was a Native American. As a teenager doing a genealogical project at school, Tonya had discovered a Métis ancestor no one had told her about. According to Uncle Aaron, she had been talking about her "Native heritage" and investing in dreamcatchers ever since.

"June," Britta said gently—she was being extra careful with me today—"listen. When I say Native American women are targeted, I don't mean that traffickers are wandering the streets hunting down women who look like they might be Native."

I shrugged and frowned. "All right."

"I mean that—June, there's a lot of poverty on the reservations. Because of hundreds of years of racism and the government screwing them over—you know all that. *That's* what these guys are looking for. Women who don't have a lot of choices. These guys aren't just snatching random women. They aren't shoving them into cars and tying them up, like in the movies . . . If they did that, people would report it. The police would get involved. No. They groom these women for a long time. Kind of break them down that way. Make them feel they got into this themselves."

"Maybe they did know Tonya. Maybe she was in Duluth those times in November and December that she went away."

"But why didn't Frank want to look for your mother in Duluth, then? Why did he think she'd be somewhere around here?"

"Well," I said, "I don't know."

"And where was her car for the last four days? If Frank drove her to Duluth?" Britta looked at me with an eyebrow raised, as if she were a teacher expecting a real answer.

I shrugged. "It was just an idea." I had been chewing hard on the pen and I realized it only when my mouth started to ache. I took the pen out of my mouth and put it back down on the desk.

On the plus side, for the last few minutes, my rash hadn't bothered me. As soon as I thought of it, it itched again.

I added huffily, "If you're so sure this didn't happen, why did you bring up all the stuff about Duluth in the first place?"

"Oh my God, June." Britta smacked her forehead as if she were a character in a cartoon.

"What?"

"I got ahead of myself. I'm sorry. My brain's all over the place. I don't think I slept at all last night. I haven't even told you the reason I started thinking about a connection to Duluth."

She told me about something that had happened at the end of December. She had found out that a druggie jam band she and Tonya liked were on tour. So she asked if Tonya wanted to go with her to see them play.

At first, Tonya had sounded interested. But when Britta told her the band was playing in Duluth, her attitude changed.

She said Duluth—Duluth? Well. Maybe. But maybe not. Maybe if it was in Fargo. But she didn't really like Duluth . . .

"What?" Britta said. "Since when?"

"Well, in the winter," Tonya had said after a pause. "All the hills. The ice. Driving there sucks. I haven't been to Duluth in ages."

Britta had laughed at her. "I don't care. I'll drive. My car's more comfortable, anyway."

I could imagine the look on Tonya's face after that comment. No, she said, more firmly. She didn't want to go.

Britta said Tonya acted funny when she pushed her on it. Why was she being so weird? Britta asked her.

She wasn't, Tonya said. She just didn't like that band that much anymore. Plus, she was short on money. She couldn't be spending what she did have on concert tickets when she still hadn't dug up enough to cover January rent.

"How surprisingly responsible of you," Britta said. "I'm impressed."

Tonya gave her a toothy smile.

"That's me. Miss Responsible," she said.

Britta left it alone after that. But she still thought there was something Tonya wasn't telling her. How many times had Tonya said "Forget bills" before, and run off with Britta or Frank or Ruby to blow her money on something fun instead?

Right after New Year's, Tonya surprised everyone by going

to work at Otten's. A few days later, she lost her license. She stopped going to work after that.

Not long after, Britta said, she was driving Tonya around one day on some errands.

Britta's car was in the shop, so they took Tonya's, an ancient black Mustang.

Britta drove Tonya to Boucher's Resort west of town. Tonya was in the resort office trying to talk the owner into giving her an advance for some work she was scheduled to do later in the month. Britta stayed in her car to check a text. Then she found some candy in her pocket. When she was putting the wrappers in the plastic bag Tonya kept on the floor of the passenger seat for garbage, she noticed something interesting in there: a receipt for a Duluth gas station, dated Christmas Day.

Britta took it out and looked at it. Then she kept digging in the bag. Alongside chip wrappers and orange peels was another piece of paper with notes on it written in pencil. Two Duluth addresses and a woman's name: Andrea.

Britta glanced out the window of the car. Tonya was still in the office. Britta could see her long red coat through the window. Her elbows on the counter, her hands in her hair.

Britta pulled a notebook out of her pocket. She wrote down the addresses and the name. Then she put the paper and the receipt back in the garbage.

When she saw Tonya heading back to the car, Britta changed her mind. She dug out the papers and handed them to Tonya.

"I thought you hated Duluth," she said.

Tonya glanced at them. She didn't look closely. But after a moment she took the papers and stuck them under her leg. Then she stared out the windshield.

"Who's Andrea?" Britta said. "Why'd you go to Duluth at Christmas?"

"I didn't. Those must be Frank's."

"That's not your handwriting?"

"Nope."

"Sure looks like it. Why did Frank take your car to Duluth?"

"Oh," Tonya said, "I don't know. To see some woman, probably."

"Andrea."

"Sure." Tonya looked out her window. "Andrea."

After Britta turned back onto the lake road, she glanced at Tonya. The pieces of paper that had been under her leg were gone. Had she put them in her pocket?

"Are you in some kind of trouble?" Britta asked.

"Nope."

"But you'd tell me if you were."

"Sure."

"If something's going on, I can help you. You and June."

"We don't need your money, rich girl," Tonya said, softening it with a smile.

"Why didn't Frank just take his truck?" Britta asked after a while.

"What?"

"To Duluth."

"That thing?" Tonya paused. "It's bad on gas."

"Well, that was nice of you. To help Frank save money on gas."

"I guess I'm a nice person." Tonya laughed.

Britta was quiet for a moment, thinking. Then she jerked her thumb back in the direction of Boucher's. "How did things go in there?"

"Oh." Tonya's laughter faded. "About how you'd imagine."

While Britta was telling me this story in the newspaper office, my phone dinged three times. Finally, I checked it.

Jack: *At yr place. Where are you?*

I started to write back, *Be at the station 10 minutes*. Then I changed "10" to "20."

"I've got to go see Jack," I told Britta. "What do you think this means?"

Britta shook her head. "Did Tonya maybe owe somebody money? Someone in Duluth? Maybe she didn't want to show her face there after this trip she took over Christmas?"

"Money for what?"

"Drugs? Maybe she'd started dealing?"

"That's what I was thinking." Triumphantly, I told her about the party Frank and Tonya had showed up at in Pluie, the one Zee had been at, too.

"Why would they go to a high-school party?" I said. "Don't you think that's weird? I was thinking that maybe, they were looking for kids to sell drugs to."

"Well." Britta tapped her finger on her lips. "I don't know. I've been to some parties in Pluie. They can be kind of—'the whole town's here,' kind of thing. More so than over here."

"That's weird. Why would you go to something like that?"

"You don't know whose house it was, do you?"

"I don't know any of those people," I said savagely.

"Well," Britta said after a minute, "Tonya could have been dealing. It's not the craziest idea."

My phone pinged again. "Okay. I should go."

"Tell me what Jack says when you're done," Britta said.

NINE

On the sidewalk, I stood squinting in the sunshine and looking at the drug store across the street. Tan brick with a grass-green awning. Some of the town's old brick structures from the early 1900s still survived on Central Avenue. Above the flat street and the low buildings stretched the white-blue sky.

I wondered what this spot had looked like before the town was built. Covered with pine trees?

Britta had made fun of me for thinking someone might have targeted Tonya because they thought she was Native. But the more I thought about it . . .

She even knew some Ojibwe. She had taught herself from a book. What if she'd been speaking it with someone she met in a bar?

As a little kid, I had thought it was neat that my mother knew another language. But after discussing the matter over with Zee when we were in high school, I found it embarrassing.

Once at the apartment I had confronted Tonya about it. I was sitting on my bed watching her clip feathers into her hair.

"I know what you are," I said to her, "you're a Pretendian."

"A what?" My mother narrowed her eyes.

"You know—like a white person who pretends to be an Indian."

"Where did you hear that?"

"A woman online."

"Well, what does she know?"

"She's a *real* Native American," I said, "a Pueblo."

On the sidewalk outside the newspaper office, I watched a few people pass. A man going into the bank. A woman holding the hand of a small child in a snowmobile suit. They didn't seem to notice me staring at them.

I thought about the things Britta had told me. Girls with unstable homes, parents who drank and used drugs. Or who were never around.

Well. None of that fit Tonya as well as it fit *me*.

Instead of going left to head back to the part of town east of the river, I turned right. The bell above the door in the hardware store clanged loudly when I pushed it open.

I knew the man at the counter a little. He was the father of one of my classmates. His mouth fell open when he saw me—he knew.

"Hi," I said, and dove quickly into the aisles before he could speak.

I found Frank looking at doorknobs and hinges. He wore a fraying knit hat and a tan canvas coat covered with splatters of gray and white. Several pieces of gold hardware gleamed in his palm. As I approached him, he closed his fingers and shook the pieces softly so that they clinked. He ran his hand over his gray-brown five-o-clock shadow, then squatted to pluck something else from a shelf.

The aisle was in the old part of the store. Here, the floors were made of planks of soft wood full of knots and creaks. Nearby was a wall of square wooden cubbyholes containing neat stacks of the stiff jeans and coveralls that the farmers wore. The newer addition of the shop, with its bright white walls and fluorescent lights, had rubber sink stoppers and dish drains arranged on wire racks.

I unwound my scarf and breathed in the metallic smell of nails and hinges. "Frank."

"Hey—Juney." Frank straightened up with a hand on his back. His arms went down to his sides, then up again, as if he were getting ready to pull me into an embrace.

The hollows under his gray eyes were so dark they looked like makeup. I put my head down and waited for the moment to pass.

"You making something?" I said.

"Gonna fix that door."

I looked at him and he said, "Your door. The bathroom door. I need something to do. You feel that way, Juney?"

"Yes."

"Your mom and I meant to get to it months ago." The tears were coming now. He didn't stop them and they caught and glistened in his chin stubble. "I don't know why we didn't. When I was growing up, my dad never would have let something like that go for so long."

"Did you learn how to build things from your dad?" I had never thought much about Frank's childhood. I tried to picture him as a little kid and failed.

"Oh, yeah. He was a master. Our place always looked good. Not because we could put a lot of money into it. We didn't need it." Frank looked proud, for a second almost happy.

"Did he do that for a living? Construction or something?"

Frank's eyes lost a little of their shine. "Oh, yeah, he did some of that. Well. I let that door go too long but I'm going to get to it now. You need your privacy, Juney."

I couldn't help myself—"Privacy?" The word came out with a sound somewhere between a laugh and a cry. "Privacy from who?"

Frank groaned. Then he seemed to be making for me again.

I said, "Frank, who's Andrea?"

He stopped coming forward and pulled his lips in tight. His eyes didn't change.

"Who?" he said.

"Andrea in Duluth."

Frank let his mouth relax open. He swung his head from side to side in an exaggerated way as if he were looking both ways before crossing a busy street. "I don't know. I don't think I know one. An Andrea."

"A friend of Tonya's, maybe?"

Frank crinkled his eyes. "Nope."

I looked at him for a while. Frank scratched his wide forehead with his free hand and turned back to the shelves.

"Do you want to know why I'm asking?" I said.

"Sure . . ."

"She's somebody Tonya knew. Or—somebody you knew? That's what Tonya said."

"That's what Tonya said?" Frank was pinching a long nail between two of his fingers. He studied it as if he'd never seen one before.

"To Britta. Tonya had her address in her car—this Andrea's. But I never heard Tonya mention her before."

"Her address?" Frank glanced at me quickly. "And where's that?"

"I told you: Duluth."

"Okay." Frank began to whistle, very softly. He tapped another doorknob with the long nail before dropping the nail back into its bin. "Well. I'm sorry, Juney. I don't know. I didn't know all of Tonya's friends. She didn't know all of mine . . ."

"You two spent a lot of time together."

"She was my best friend."

His tone had changed. He wasn't lying or hiding anything there.

My phone was vibrating again in my pocket. I turned away without even saying goodbye, left Frank with his grief, and walked away with mine.

But my own grief felt imperfect and even impure next to grubby Frank's. It was a relief to again fling myself out into the cold, bright air.

Only moments after I did, a squad car pulled up beside me. Jack.

"June," he said, after lowering the passenger side window, "there you are."

When I peered in at him, Jack didn't look the same to me as he had before yesterday. I thought he was looking at me differently, too. There was a strange formality between us, as if we had met only a few days before.

But also as if, at that first encounter, something had passed between us. An understanding of some kind.

It made me feel oddly shy. But somehow, at the same time, bold.

"Am I late?" I looked at my phone. Only then did I notice that while I had drafted my message to Jack, I had forgotten to send it. "Sorry . . ."

"I was worried." Jack looked exasperated, and the circles under his blue eyes were almost as dark as Frank's. "When you weren't home this morning, and Zee and Aaron didn't know where you'd gone—"

"Why were you worried?" My tone sounded new and strange even to me. Sharp. Almost saucy.

Jack was getting sharper, too. "Get in the car, okay? I need to talk to you at the station."

"Can I go home first? I want to see Uncle Aaron."

"June. I've spent the last hour looking for you. Get in, please."

"Do I have to?"

"What do you think? This is an investigation."

Tricky, tricky . . . Even I knew I couldn't trust my knowledge of the law. Everything I knew stemmed from historical British cop dramas.

At the station, Jack pulled out my chair in the interrogation room before I could stop him. He asked if I were comfortable. Did I want any tea or coffee or a snack or anything?

I started to say no. It felt right to be clean and empty today.

My stomach rumbled at this inopportune moment. I felt a little dizzy, too. "Actually—"

Jack jumped up and left the room. He came back with two cups of coffee and a tray of rolls and about seven little packets of butter.

I started to cut a roll in half and Jack just sat there and watched me. I could see him trying not to look at the red bumps traveling up my throat.

"Don't worry," I said, tapping my neck, "it's just the usual. It's not the measles or anything."

"I know that." He sounded annoyed.

"You can go ahead. I'm ready."

"I'd rather you ate first."

"Jack."

"All right." He sighed. "June, they were able to do an autopsy last night. Everything they found points to suicide."

I took a bite of roll and chewed it slowly. Then I put the rest of it back down on the tray.

"Everything?"

"The gun was hers. We talked about that last night. They also found gunpowder residue on her hand consistent with her pulling the trigger herself."

"What else?"

Jack leaned forward in his chair. "June, you don't need all the details."

I leaned forward in my own chair. I picked up the rest of the roll and put it in my mouth and chewed.

"Don't I?" I said.

Jack sighed. "The angle of the gun—everything. And there was no sign anyone else was even there. We've got your footprints. Frank's. The tracks from Frank's truck. That's it."

"So not even Tonya's tracks."

"No. Too much snow came down."

"So someone else *could* have been there."

"Yes . . ."

"How long was she dead when we found her?"

"About ten, fifteen hours. They think."

"Did you find any fibers on her clothes?"

"You've been watching a lot of crime shows."

"But did you?"

"We're doing our job, June."

"It sounds like your mind's already made up."

"Well—"

"Did you talk to Frank?"

"Of course we did."

"Did you ask him how he knew Tonya would be there?"

"He said he didn't know for sure."

"Well, of course he would *say*—"

"But this piece of land that he brought you to," Jack cut in. "You said you had never been there before?"

"No. I mean, not that I know of."

"But did you know about it?"

"Know what about it?"

"That your mother owned it?"

I just sat there and looked at him for a minute. "What?"

"You didn't know," Jack said.

Slowly I shook my head. "What do you mean? Did someone give it to her or something?"

And, more importantly, *had* Tonya actually left me something? A resource? A legacy? Not the family farm south of Bagwajipin. But something. A piece of land—in the woods that she treasured so much?

Jack must have guessed what I was thinking. He said quickly, "June, I'm sorry, but—the land was something your mom and Frank bought together. About ten years ago. And it belongs to him now."

"What? Why?"

"They arranged it legally so that if one of them died, his or her share went to the other."

I rubbed my forehead with my hand, then grabbed another roll and buttered it.

"Well," I said bitterly, "Tonya's just full of surprises, isn't she."

Jack told me that when Randy, the sheriff, asked Frank what the land was for, he said they had bought it for hunting. I shook my head. Tonya didn't hunt, I told Jack. She didn't like it.

But at the same time, I felt tired all of the sudden of looking for signs and symbols and clues. What was the point? Who was I doing it for? Tonya? For a mother who had left her only valuable possession to her degenerate friend instead of to her own penniless daughter?

Jack said, "Frank hunts. And they had started to build a deer stand in one of the trees. I saw it this morning."

I shrugged. "Okay." I was failing to see why any of this mattered. I wanted more than ever to go see my uncle. I closed my eyes and leaned back in my chair, scratching the rash on my chest through my sweater.

Then Jack told me that they had questioned Frank last night about why he had seemed worried or afraid to go to that spot last night.

"Oh, yeah?" I opened my eyes again. "What did he say?"

"That was what I wanted to run by you. Frank told us he was afraid. He said he thought if Tonya was there, she would be dead. Because she had told him that if she was ever sick and about to die, she wanted to go there. He thought she might go there to—"

"She wasn't sick," I interrupted him. "Wait—was she sick?"

"No, there's nothing to indicate—"

"So why didn't Frank want me to get out of the truck?"

"He says he didn't want you to see her like that. He says that when he found his own father dead—"

"But that's not true. When we were at the apartment, Frank was begging me to come with him. Saying he couldn't do it alone."

"I guess at that point he still thought you might find her alive?"

I shook my head. "No. He's lying. Why would he lie?"

"Maybe, when the time came, he changed his mind? Decided he wanted to protect you? Does that sound like something Frank would do?"

I thought about it. Protect me? Frank, in his way, had always done some "father things" for me. Taught me how to drive. Come to my choir concerts. Sometimes even when Tonya herself didn't bother to come.

I was always embarrassed when Frank showed up at school. Or when I was downtown with some of the other kids and he came up to say hello. Wearing some old sweatshirt with an oil stain across the front. Or something even grosser. A smear of orange sauce, still fresh. With alcohol on his breath.

Jack and I sat for a moment in silence.

"Could someone have forced her to pull the trigger?" I asked him.

"Well—why? How?"

"She was in trouble. And she knew something that would get someone else in trouble. So whoever it was, they threatened her."

"With what?"

"To hurt someone she knew. Me? Even Frank. Couldn't that explain why he was scared?"

"Of course it's possible . . ."

"They didn't find any signs of sexual assault, did they?"

"They didn't," Jack said quietly.

"What about drugs?"

"No drugs. Not even any alcohol. Why do you ask?"

I told him everything Britta and I had talked about this

morning. When I was done, he said, "It's an interesting theory, June."

"And not completely out of nowhere, right?"

"But, without any sign of rape or drugs—"

"Yes. I know."

"Tonya didn't even use her bank or credit card in the last three days. Not in Duluth. Not anywhere."

"That doesn't prove anything. She didn't have any money in the bank."

"Okay, June," Jack said. "I'll bring all this to Randy. He'll call Britta if he thinks it's worth looking into. If he decides it is, we'll look into it."

"Well. I would hope so. Since it's your job," I said.

TEN

I called Britta on my walk home.

"I'm sorry, June. That must have been hard to hear," she said.

"But what do you think about this?" I told her my theory about the forced suicide. Someone could have made Tonya write the note, I said.

Britta mused, "Yes, that would explain the signature . . ." I was quiet. "But this morning we were just speculating. The evidence—"

"We have evidence. Frank acting strange. Tonya lying."

"Those are more like questions."

"Duluth," I said. "Duluth."

"Yes, though we don't have a solid way to even connect Duluth to your mother's death."

"Not yet."

"What do you have in mind, June?"

I was home by then and I didn't want to continue the conversation in front of Uncle Aaron and Zee. I also didn't want to stand out in the cold, so I promised Britta I'd call her later.

In the apartment, Uncle Aaron and Zee were sitting at one end of the kitchen table eating breakfast, Zee still in pajamas, her short blond hair standing in peaks and tufts all over her head, her bare feet on the seat of her chair.

Uncle Aaron stood up when I came in.

"There you are," he said.

He was already combed and dressed. Uncle Aaron had straight hair the ash-brown color of mine and my mother's; he wore it down to his chin, but always smooth and neatly trimmed. He looked like a teddy bear with his short dark beard, his pudgy belly in a soft sweater, and the warm, worried gaze he turned on me.

For a second, the cozy scene, the sweet and buttery smell of cinnamon toast, made me feel warm and fuzzy, too.

Until I noticed something amiss in the room.

For one thing, another smell was lurking behind the fragrant one. Something acrid. I hadn't emptied the litterbox yesterday or today. Poor Enid!

And there was something else. A conspiratorial feeling in the air.

The partially filled-out college application forms I had been keeping on my nightstand had been moved to the kitchen table.

I didn't go to the table right away, but let Uncle Aaron come to me. He hugged me and began to cry.

I stiffened. I had thought seeing Uncle Aaron—perhaps my only unsullied ally in what felt today like a debauched and ugly world—might be the blow that finally splintered the dam.

But I felt sharp, tight, intact. My mind was zipping and buzzing as if it had been plugged in.

"It's okay to cry, June," he said.

"So I see," I murmured.

He pulled back and gave me a tender look. I felt myself wishing he had slapped me instead.

"Don't do that. Don't be nice to me when . . . I can't stand it," I said.

My Uncle Aaron, who had told me about a memory that always made me sad: it was from the day after his parents' death, before he moved to the Cities to live with Aunt Sylvi and Uncle Rich. He was in the farmhouse on County 82 with Tonya. He headed out on the dark frosty morning to tend to the animals, a small boy lugging cumbersome buckets of feed all by himself. Then he came in sweaty and tired to help Tonya nurse a hangover with coffee and chicken soup.

Since I could remember, I had been having phone conversations with Uncle Aaron two or three times a week. I would tell him everything that was happening in my life, with Zee, with my classes, with Tonya. He listened carefully, talked through things with me. I asked him for advice. I relied on him. I loved him terribly.

We were alike in a lot of ways. Sometimes too alike.

When I was still a little kid, but started to really complain about Tonya, the stress of worrying about her, and about whether we would get kicked out of the apartment next month, or if she would remember to bring home cereal that evening so that I could eat breakfast before I went to school, Uncle Aaron began to say, "Maybe you should come live here, June."

"Here": his home in south Minneapolis. It *was* my kind of place. A two-bedroom apartment in a 1920s brownstone building. Dark wood trim and a clawfoot tub. Cast-iron radiators. Built-in bookshelves and shiny hardwood floors. Always clean and neat.

Zee liked it, too. The two of us had driven down to visit Uncle Aaron last summer. Zee loved being in the city. The music and the theater, the coffeeshops and restaurants. The goths, the punks. The woman who did the local TV news in androgynous suits and a curly pompadour.

Zee did all the driving while we were there. She loved that, too, picking up on the fly how to zip in and out of all that traffic and understand the significance of an array of bewildering signs and signals and lights. I got flustered just trying to walk across Uncle Aaron's busy street.

Go live with Uncle Aaron? Even as a small child, I had seriously considered it.

There came a day when I tested Tonya with the idea. It wasn't a nice memory. I remember it very clearly.

I was eleven. Tonya was getting ready to go out somewhere that night. I assumed to some kind of party. She didn't just toss on a flannel and pull her hair back, as she would do when she went to Berg's or Tamarack to play pool with Ruby. She put on her nicest slim jeans. Lipstick. Hooked a silver choker with a turquoise charm around her neck. She looked pretty. It didn't take many of these little touches for Tonya, in her early thirties at this point, to look as if she had just graduated from high school.

Probably I should have been used to being left alone. Certainly Tonya thought so. But we had just watched the movie *Mama* together, curled up on her bed. I was terrified. An evil spirit following two little girls from the deep woods into a neat and civilized house? I couldn't imagine anything worse.

I cried. I begged her not to go.

"Please not tonight. I don't want to be alone."

"Aw, baby." Tonya stopped applying blush long enough to touch my hair. I was standing beside her, watching her in the mirror. We had the same big hazel eyes spaced far apart and heart-shaped faces. Her skin was gold while mine was pink, but I had her thick and wavy brown hair.

"I hate scary movies about the woods."

"The woods aren't scary. They're just the woods. And they'll always give you what you need and protect you. That's what that movie's about, you know."

I stared at her. I didn't think that sounded right, but what did I know?

"Besides, you're in town. The woods can't get you here." Tonya grinned at me in the mirror.

"They're right there." I pointed out the window. Tonya knew very well that Aulneau gave in to the wilderness less than a mile away.

"Call Zee. She'll come over. Or you could go over there."

"She's in Wisconsin with her family."

I had been hanging on to Tonya, clutching her silky blouse; but now I went to sit on my bed. She was combing her long hair. The longer I watched her, the more my fear hardened into anger.

After a while, I said, "That movie was really scary."

"Mm." Tonya was checking her phone.

"I don't think you should have let me watch it."

Tonya smiled. "Well. It looks like you're probably right."

"Uncle Aaron wouldn't have let me."

"No—that's definitely true."

"Uncle Aaron says that maybe I should come live with him," I said.

As I kept watching Tonya, I began to shake. It wasn't because of the movie anymore.

Tonya was quiet for a few minutes. Her eyes were on the floor. Slowly, she put her phone in her pocket and picked up her denim jacket from where it was lying across the end of her bed.

"I know," she said quietly.

I had a cold feeling in my stomach. I felt as if my teeth were about to chatter, though it was a nice spring night. The sound of birds, and a breeze that smelled of mud and melting snow, were coming in through the tattered window screen.

"Well," I said after a few torturous minutes, "do you think I should?"

Tonya was still looking at the floor. When she finally spoke again, her voice was even softer.

"That's up to you, June," she said.

For a moment I couldn't breathe. My chest ached. Then I looked down as well, exhaling slowly. I stared at the pattern on my bedspread between my crossed legs: small purple flowers on a light green background. The blanket matched the one on my mother's bed.

I decided in that moment that this coming September, for my twelfth birthday, I would ask Uncle Aaron for something different. Neat and stylish stripes.

He came through. He always did. An Art Deco pattern. Gray, blush pink, brown. A thin pinstripe of black. The material was heavy and expensive. He probably paid way too much for it in the kind of trendy store in the Cities he would never go to for himself.

Tonya was putting on her shoes. Then she was standing over me. She put her hand on my head.

"All right," she said. "I have to go now, Juney."

"Well. You don't *have* to," I said.

Eight years later, I pulled out of my hug with Uncle Aaron and looked behind him at my bed. The bedspread was still in excellent shape. Other than the black walnut dresser with antique handles that my Uncle Rich had made me, that blanket was the loveliest thing in the dumpy room.

After that conversation with Tonya—in which I came face-to-face with the extent of her indifference, and became determined to punish her for it with my everlasting presence—whenever Uncle Aaron again brought up the possibility of me leaving Tonya's apartment, I would say, "I guess I shouldn't. She'd starve without me. And she'd never remember to brush her teeth."

Uncle Aaron kept trying. Finally, after I entered high school, his mantra changed to, "Well, it'll only be a couple years now, anyway," assuming without asking, as Zee always did, that I was dying to flee to the city and would fly gratefully out of town the moment I graduated, never looking back.

Now that Tonya was dead, Uncle Aaron had lost everyone in his immediate family. He was really going to want me to come live with him now.

I sat down at the table with him and Zee. I glanced at the college application forms. I saw that wasn't the only thing there—

there were also three checks. For the month's rent and utilities. The amount for the rent was written in neatly, while the amounts for the gas and electric were blank.

I was embarrassed and didn't mention it. But I picked up the application forms off the tabletop covered with hundreds of coffee rings. I folded the papers in half and put them in my lap. Zee sneaked an uneasy look at Uncle Aaron.

"So, you guys found something to eat?" I said and wiped my uncle's tears off my face with the back of my hand.

I took off my scarf. Zee said, "Oh, man, June. It looks worse than it did last night." I ran my finger lightly over my throat.

Uncle Aaron said, "Don't worry. I figured that. I picked up the arnica cream on my way out of the Cities."

I ducked into the bathroom and looked in the mirror. "I know it looks bad. But it's actually feeling better." It had itched only intermittently this morning. More so when my mind was unoccupied.

I glanced at the broken bathroom door leaning against the wall on my way out. Frank was right. Doing something helped.

I sat down at the table across from Uncle Aaron. I looked at him and realized I was going to have to tell him the news: what they had found out in the autopsy.

Before I could get myself to start, he said, "I know. I talked to Jack this morning."

Zee stood up and came around the table and hugged me from behind. I closed my eyes. In the warm, shaky, sobby darkness of Zee's muscular arms wrapped tightly around me, I heard Uncle Aaron begin to say the kinds of things I imagined everyone had to say when someone committed suicide.

"Just remember that your mother loved you. And this isn't your fault. This isn't anyone's fault. Don't start thinking that the last thing you said to her was so terrible . . . that you should have said—whatever it was. 'I love you.' Don't start thinking that if you had, if she had known how much you loved her . . ."

I wondered what the last thing Uncle Aaron had said to Tonya had been. "She knew how much you loved her," I said softly.

Uncle Aaron tucked a strand of dark hair behind his ear. He took off his glasses and laid them on the table and covered his face with his hands.

"Why did she do it?" he said.

"I don't know. But I think Frank knows something."

"That wouldn't surprise me."

His voice was quick and sharp. Zee had gone back to her chair a few moments before. Now she looked anxious again. She avoided my gaze and coughed and shifted in her seat.

Uncle Aaron said, "I told him to stay away from her."

"Why?"

"Do you have to ask, June? That jerk?"

"Well." I felt strangely defensive of Frank. He was a lot of things, but . . .

"I bet he's never worked a full day in his life."

"He did at Otten's. Isn't that where they met? Before I was born?"

"At Otten's . . . about a hundred years ago."

"You can say the same thing about Tonya. Maybe she was the bad influence on *him*. Who knows?"

Uncle Aaron shook his head darkly.

"*I* know," he said.

"What do you mean?"

"Just leave it alone, June."

"Do you think Frank was selling drugs?"

"I wouldn't doubt it. Listen, June," Uncle Aaron said before I could speak, "I know that Britta and Jack are looking into some things. That's fine. I guess we'll have to know the truth in the end."

"*Have* to? Don't you want to?"

"Yes. Of course. But can you stay out of it? And can we not talk about it right now?"

"If Tonya was—"

"I don't want to think about my sister being mixed up in any of that stuff."

"Mixed up in it? I'm talking about her being a victim."

"Well. Okay. But I don't want to talk about it. Not today. Not right now. All right? I know her life was a mess. You think I don't know that? But she was my sister. I grew up with her. She was— you know. She was sweet. Funny. In many ways, a good person. She was friendly to people. She loved nature. You and I, June, we don't need to be thinking about that other stuff. That's what the police are for. We've got other things to think about . . ."

I had been dreading this part. Arrangements. A memorial. Of course, Uncle Aaron, earnest and kind, generous and hospitable, a wonderful cook and giver of dinner parties, a worried hen who loved to keep everyone around him comfortable, warm, and well-fed, would want to put his energy there: into the right place and time, the most meaningful food and flowers. The right people, music that fit the occasion. The perfect words to say. He was already coming up with those.

As Uncle Aaron started to list people to call and cookies to bake, I had an idea. I got up and began pulling photo albums from the bookshelf. In the closet, I moved aside a pile of Tonya's gauzy scarves—Indian pashminas in red and copper, a magenta tie-dyed number featuring a psychedelic owl with fiery eyes—to get to a shoebox on the back shelf.

Uncle Aaron stopped talking to watch me. "What are you doing, June?"

"Pictures. For the memorial."

And both Uncle Aaron and Zee—who, I remembered only now, should have been in school, but instead was diligently transcribing notes for Uncle Aaron on a piece of notebook paper—looked relieved and satisfied.

An hour later, I convinced Zee to go to school. I knew she had a rehearsal for vocal ensemble contests that day. She had a perfect piping soprano, pure and sincere, like an urchin singing for his supper in a Dickens special on public TV. While Zee was getting dressed and doing her hair behind the bathroom curtain—she kept a spare can of sculpting wax in there for such occasions—I put together a foil package of trail mix and peanut butter crackers and tucked it into her leather messenger bag. It wasn't *entirely* unfair that kids at school called us husband and wife.

After she left, Uncle Aaron and I did the dishes. Then we sat down and looked at each other. Enid fell asleep in a sunny patch on the carpet.

I couldn't sit still. I stood up and began to walk around the room. I changed Enid's litter box. I found this month's electric and gas bills and wrote in the amounts on Uncle Aaron's checks.

I sat down on Tonya's bed and began to page through her journals again. I could feel Uncle Aaron watching me.

I looked up. "What's the matter?"

"Are those your mother's? What are you looking for?"

"Maybe a quote or something, to use for the memorial?"

This time, however, the excuse didn't fly.

"Why don't you let me do that?" Uncle Aaron came over to the bed and picked up a stack of books. He hugged them to his chest and brought them back with him to the rocking chair.

I watched him. "Why?"

"Listen, June, it might be emotional. With your rash and all . . . why don't you just relax? Have a cup of tea? Or, if you want something to do," he went on, very carefully, "what about your college application forms? Zee said they're due in three weeks. Less than that. Today's the 12th, you know."

"Wait a minute," I said. "You think I'm going to fill out college application forms *today*?"

"Not today—no. Of course not today. Unless you really wanted to. But soon, maybe?"

"You know I haven't decided yet about college."

"June. You can't be thinking of staying here now."

"Now? You mean now that Tonya's gone?"

"Well." Uncle Aaron had one of Tonya's notebooks open in his lap, but he hadn't read a word. He looked down at it now.

"I thought the whole point was that you wanted me to get away from her."

"Not to get away from her." Uncle Aaron frowned at the scrawled page. "No. Not to get away. Just to have more support. More structure."

"You could come here."

"June, you know, with my life, my job . . ."

It was a conversation we'd had many times. I did understand. Uncle Aaron loved his apartment and his pretty neighborhood and his job as a nurse in a care center for old people. He loved old people. He was good with them. Most of them were pliable in response to his sweetness, and even if they weren't, he found them fairly easy to manage. Their needs were simple most of the time. They couldn't move fast and they couldn't get far. Unlike Tonya, who was always slipping out of his grasp.

Move back here? I could tell he'd always been afraid of the idea. Of being drawn back into Tonya's chaos, as he had been as a child.

Poor Uncle Aaron—how he hated chaos and disorder! Once, when Zee and I were staying with him, I saw him fret and almost cry when he couldn't find the knife he usually used to cut his meatloaf. After doing the dishes, Zee had accidentally put it in the wrong drawer. It goes without saying that any of his other knives would have worked perfectly fine.

I worried about that kind of obsessiveness rubbing off on me. I didn't think it would take much for me to go there. I didn't want to be my flaky mother; but I didn't want to be exactly like Uncle Aaron, either.

But now? I could stay in the apartment and Uncle Aaron

could get a job in town as a nurse and buy a house. They were cheap here.

It was a nice town. Quiet and friendly. And in the summer, with all the tourists, it was festive and fun. We could go to events at the school together. Take picnics to the lake. I could see Uncle Aaron getting into town politics. I wouldn't mind getting involved with the historical society. Find out more about our family.

Jack would be here . . .

Maybe that's what I wanted? Maybe not?

"Well," I ventured, "it would be different now."

Uncle Aaron looked around the room. At the dilapidated furniture, the yellow curtain, the broken bathroom door. He looked out the window at the one car driving by on the street.

"June, it just doesn't make a lot of sense," he said. "For me *or* for you. Zee's not going to be here. What do you have here?"

"The paper. Why waste money learning how to become a journalist when I'm already getting paid to be a journalist?"

"You're a typist, June."

"I write the School News."

"Not after you graduate you won't. And don't worry about the money. You'll get loans, then you'll pay them off. That's what I did."

"I'm sick of it. I'm sick of owing money."

"You don't owe anybody money. Do you?" Uncle Aaron wrinkled his brow and leaned towards me in the rocking chair. It groaned.

I shrugged. "Tonya—"

"No. Those are your mother's debts. Not yours." Uncle Aaron screwed up his face and scratched his hair. He took off his glasses and put them on again. "Listen, June. I don't like hearing you talk this way about money. That's not something you should be worrying about right now. Getting money, how you're going to get it . . . That's what would be so great about you going to college now. Your mother didn't have anything, you don't have anything, so you'll do well on financial aid. If you go to college, you'll get loans, and then you won't have to think about money for a while. I'll help you with living expenses. Maybe you'll even live with me—if you'd like that. I know I would. And then when you graduate, okay. At that point, you're ready to get a good job. That's when you can start thinking about money. Okay?"

"Tonya never gave enough thought to money. And look at what happened to her."

"You're not your mother," Uncle Aaron said.

ELEVEN

On Saturday, Zee arrived at our door with her hair slicked flat. She wore the same slim black suit that had driven our choir teacher nearly mad when Zee showed up in it for the choir festival this fall.

"It's just a dress; would it kill you to wear one?" Mrs. Beasley had cried.

"You'd say that if one of the boys showed up in a dress?"

Mrs. Beasley had accused Zee, in her sober, simple black, of hankering for special attention. Our illustrious choral leader, herself clad in a tiered nylon affair of bubblegum pink, hadn't been thrilled with my choice, either: pulled from an ancient box, wrapped in even more ancient brown tissue paper, my great-great-great grandmother Bergeron's glittering flapper dress. Heavy black silk covered in sequins, beads, and fringe, with satiny gloves and a pair of strappy black heels to match.

To my uncle's horror, I had considered that dress again today, for the memorial. But the plunging neckline showed not only my voluminous cleavage but my rash in all its glory—fading and no longer itchy, but still ugly. I opted for Tonya's mother's black dress with a stiff flared skirt, three-quarter sleeves, and white Peter Pan collar.

"You look beautiful, June," Zee said when I opened the door.

We liked clothes, Zee and me. We liked rummage sales and online vintage shops. Clothes "made the man"—no one knew that better than we did.

At the service, Mrs. Beasley had to watch Zee sing in the suit and she couldn't do a thing about it. Flanked by two tenors from our small high-school choir, Zee took the melody in "Bridge over Troubled Water." Tonya's favorite song.

I cried, then, for the first time. I couldn't tell if it was for my mother or not.

Uncle Aaron had picked a biodegradable urn. A small brown box we would set out on the water when the summer came. I stared at it. Tonya was in there, smaller than ever. I couldn't really believe it.

I was proud of Uncle Aaron. He *had* gotten everything right. The service was mostly silence. We listened to a recording of birds chirping in a forest. There was a stream, too. Occasionally, a rush of wind blew through the trees.

A few people came up to say a few words. Tonya's friend Ruby, who in tight ripped jeans told a few tasteless stories I could have lived without.

Most everyone from my grade was there. That was a nice surprise.

When it was over, I mingled, as one is supposed to do. Zee's parents. Her mother, tall and thin, who worked at the grocery store, her father an inch shorter, wearing a jacket embroidered with his name, Jake, and the emblem of his garage. They were nice enough people. Though I didn't love the way they treated Zee, especially in public: as if they were embarrassed of her. Her mother still called her Suzanne, while her father had settled on "Kid."

In this way, Tonya had been better. She never acted as if Zee were different than anybody else. Often she had told Zee how much she liked her style.

When Zee had her trouble with Mrs. Beasley, her father said, "Do whatever you're gonna do. But if you want things, sometimes you're gonna have to play by other people's rules . . ."

At the choir festival, Mrs. Beasley was so furious with Zee

that she didn't let her sing. Well. The joke was on her. The so-pranos were terrified. They relied heavily on Zee. They pan-icked and sounded atrocious.

After the service, Zee's parents stood a few feet away from Zee when the two of us went up to greet them. They didn't look at her even as they murmured in agreement with me: Yes, she had sounded beautiful. Yes, it was a nice thing for her to do. I linked my arm with my friend's and steered her away.

I floated through the afternoon. I talked to some kids from school.

Ms. Karbo came. She sat at a table in the reception room with Carla Vincent. Carla's cinnamon-brown hair was braided into a knot at the base of her neck and held in place with a pearl pin.

Ms. Karbo gave me a hug. "When are you coming back to school, June? Next week?"

"Probably." I did miss Ms. Karbo's anatomy class. She was good at coming up with tangible metaphors to explain com-plicated concepts. Right now, we were on the nervous system, and soon we would move on to infection and disease. Maybe somewhere in those chapters was some information Ms. Karbo would transform into poetry I could internalize into a preventa-tive against these pesky rashes.

"It won't be easy. But it'll help to have something to put your mind on."

I nodded. Carla said to me, "I'm sorry about your mom. She was a nice person."

"Thank you." I wanted to ask Carla if she had minded about Tonya being a Pretendian, sitting in the café where Carla was a waitress with her beaded purse and Kokopellis in her ears. But I figured it wasn't a great idea.

"She always left a tip," Carla said. "Not everybody does that."

Zee approached the table, looking shy, like ninth-grade Zee again. She stopped to talk to another girl from school and Carla watched them. Her small bow mouth was carefully painted with mauve lipstick. I felt touched that my classmates had gone to all this effort for me.

Ms. Karbo went to the drink table for coffee. She was wearing tall brown boots and thick tights with stripes that matched her dark-rimmed glasses. She was so stylish, Ms. Karbo.

"Thank you for coming. I like your pin," I said to Carla, pointing to her hair.

"Thanks. Listen, June." Carla turned to me and sat back in her chair. "Can I talk to you about something? About Zee? Or would it be weird," she said, looking suddenly abashed, "today . . ."

"No." I was curious. "What about Zee?"

"Does she think I'm prejudiced against, like, gay people or whatever, and that's why I haven't wanted to be in your club?"

"Zee likes the term 'queer,'" I said importantly.

"Okay—queer. But I don't have a problem with that."

"Okay . . ."

"Something just bugs me. Maybe it shouldn't. I don't know. I know Zee isn't different because she chooses to be. But it's, like—she could take it off if she wanted to. Pretend not to be."

"She shouldn't have to, though."

"I'm not saying she should. I'm just trying to explain . . . I can't take off who *I* am—pretend I'm someone different—even if I wanted to. But she *could*—you see what I mean?"

"I know it might seem that way," I said slowly, "but it's not. It's who she *is*."

"I know that. You're not listening," said Carla.

Ms. Karbo came back to the table then and Carla and I looked away from each other. For some reason, Carla didn't want to have this conversation in front of Ms. Karbo any more than I did.

I saw then that Frank was in the room, coming into the reception area from the chapel. He stopped and said a word to Zee. She put her chin in the air and turned her back on him.

Now he was coming towards our table. As I was getting up to go meet him, I felt a hand on my arm.

Carla said, low, "June, please don't tell Zee what I said. I shouldn't have. I know what it's like to feel like you're all alone."

I shrugged. "Sure. No problem."

When I reached Frank, I tried to hide my surprise: "You look nice," I said.

He had on new shoes and a well-fitting charcoal suit. It looked brand-new. Sometime in the last few days, he must have driven all the way to Ziibi or Hinhan to buy it.

Frank looked gratified. "I'm glad you like it, Juney."

"How are you doing?"

"Oh," Frank said, looking down at the dark carpet in his shambly way, "I'm not gonna lie."

"Frank—" I began.

"Juney, maybe you could tell me what that address was. I was thinking, if it turned out I knew the place, I might be able to tell you more about it."

"The address. You mean the woman you didn't know—Andrea?"

"The woman—yeah."

"Do you know Duluth pretty well, Frank?"

"Oh. You know. I know some people there."

"And Tonya did, too?"

"Oh yeah," Frank said slowly. "Tonya, too."

"I don't have it. I'll ask Britta if she remembers it offhand."

I looked around the chapel, then in the reception room. I had seen Britta in there when I was talking to Carla, but I didn't see her now. People were still in there eating turkey on buttered buns and Snicker salad. As I walked back, Frank watched me uneasily.

"If you think it would help. If not, don't worry about it . . ."

Frank was looking around the room, too. We saw Jack at the same time, heading our way. He was threading through the blond wood pews in a dark blue sweater that matched his eyes. Seeing him, Frank pouted, wiped his nose, and took a few steps away as if getting ready to run.

"Frank, if you're in some kind of trouble—" I started to say.

"Don't," he said in a low voice.

"Are you afraid of someone?"

Frank still wouldn't look at me. I looked at the bald spot on the top of his head.

"Stop sniffing around, Juney," he muttered.

"What? Why? Tell me."

"No. I promised your mother."

"What?"

I could hear the alarm in my own voice. I felt the people nearest us—the funeral director, Uncle Aaron, Aunt Sylvi and Uncle Rich, the everlasting Ruby—turn to look. Frank glanced up at me quickly, too.

"Frank? What didn't Tonya want me to know?"

Precisely at the moment Jack arrived, Frank hurried away. Jack watched him go.

"What was all that about? You look great, June."

He looked good, too. I looked at the dark curls around his ears. I said impatiently, "He admitted he knows something. He just won't tell me what it is."

Jack was carrying a plastic bag. I looked down at it, then up at him. His eyes looked faintly hurt.

"Your mom's things," he said and handed it to me.

I opened the handles. Her wallet. Her smartphone. I had told Jack we didn't want her clothes. Some of them had blood on them.

"You don't want to keep looking at these?"

"We got what we needed from them. There's nothing on her phone. She didn't have another one, did she, June?"

"Another phone? No."

"Okay. Her wallet is mostly full of leaves."

"What?"

"Pressed ones. I thought you might like to keep them?"

I peered in the bag and shook it a little. "What about her keys? The car?"

"Well," Jack said.

"So you are still looking at that?"

"Is that going to be a problem, June?"

"No," I said slowly, thinking.

"I can take you anywhere you need to go. Have you been back to school yet?"

"This means you haven't closed it?" I said. "Her case?"

"Well. No. We haven't."

"Good."

"It'll be hard, June, but go back to school. It'll help to have something else on your mind."

"I will."

"It was like that when my dad died. Listen, June. I need to come by and look around the apartment. Look at your mother's things. Those journals you were talking about? Can I come by tonight?"

"Sure. Of course. Just text me later."

"What are you doing now?"

"Oh, you know . . . family . . ." It was a good excuse to start moving away. And Aunt Sylvi was coming towards me, anyway, bless her! Being around Jack made me feel strangely agitated. "Thank you, Jack. And thank you for coming."

Jack looked injured again.

"Well—of course, June," he said.

Aunt Sylvi stood aside politely and waited for him to go. Then she came in for a hug. Aunt Sylvi was my grandfather's sister. She had the Ravndalens' bright blue eyes and small, bird-like stature. I bent down like a giant to carefully envelop her

111

fragile bones, encased in a subtle cloud of her English rose perfume.

"He's cute." She nodded discreetly as Jack walked away. Aunt Sylvi loved to allude to my romantic affairs, as non-existent as they were.

"He is. But no." I shook my head and smiled.

Aunt Sylvi smiled, too. "I talked to your friend Zee. She's a sweetie. Are you two—?"

"No. Everyone just thinks we are."

Even though she was in her late seventies, and had silver hair going thin on top and a bum knee and ankle that made her walk crookedly, even with a cane, Aunt Sylvi giggled like a girl.

"I can't help it. You kids are so darling, June."

I loved my Great-Aunt Sylvi and Great-Uncle Rich, who had taken Uncle Aaron in when he was small and tried to do what they could for Tonya. They lived in a suburb of Minneapolis, in a house crammed with craft supplies, work benches, power tools, and sewing machines. Several summers I had spent a week or two there. On one of my visits, Aunt Sylvi had taught me freehand embroidery so I could embellish my clothes.

During the service, Aunt Sylvi had hobbled to the front of the room to speak about Tonya: her free spirit and her gentleness. She described the way Tonya had learned from Uncle Rich how to use a table saw, and how she had a real talent for refurbishing busted old furniture.

"June, I'd like to talk to you for a minute," Aunt Sylvi said now.

"Sure."

"It'll be hard to get you alone at the apartment. Would you help me carry some things to the car?"

As we walked towards the door that led to the parking lot of the funeral home, me balancing a pile of silver trays covered in cracker crumbs, I saw Uncle Aaron watching us.

"Aunt Sylvi—where are you going?" He stood at the front of the reception room, a coffee pot in his hand.

Aunt Sylvi held up a hand and waved without looking back. She crept intently towards the door.

"We'll be back in a minute," I called to him.

Outside, the wind was strong and cold. Aunt Sylvi buried her little chin in her collar. At the car, she got in the driver's seat and asked me to get in the passenger's side. When I did, she turned to me and clasped my hand. Her skin was surprisingly soft, her grip alarmingly firm.

"June, I want you to brace yourself."

"Okay." I stared at her.

A strange feeling came over me. My heart began to beat fast. I had the sudden sensation that I had fallen into the water and Aunt Sylvi's elderly grip was the only thing keeping me from sinking. Or that I'd gone over the side of a cliff and my feet were dangling in the air.

These feelings seemed more real than reality . . . The car, the parking lot. Aunt Sylvi about to speak.

About what? I wanted to prepare. Brace myself? But how?

"Okay," I said again.

Aunt Sylvi said, "Your Uncle Aaron would rather I didn't tell you. But I'm afraid, June, the way things are going, that some things could come out soon about your mother. I think it would be best if you heard them from the family."

"Right . . ."

"I'm sorry I'm only telling you now. Maybe you deserved to know earlier. But we had to leave it up to Tonya. It was her story."

"Is this about my father?"

"Well"—Aunt Sylvi sighed—"in a way."

She described how, when Tonya got pregnant with me at the age of twenty, she came to Aunt Sylvi. She wanted help and advice. She said she had been lying to Aunt Sylvi and Uncle Rich for a year. She hadn't been supporting herself solely by mowing lawns and mending fences.

Aunt Sylvi used the word "escort." I was confused at first.

"You mean, like, helping an old person?" I was thinking of attendants and paid companions in a Brontë novel—perhaps optimistically so.

"No. I mean dates. With a man. But not really dates," said Aunt Sylvi, delicate to the end.

TWELVE

"*In any case,*"

I read aloud as I typed on my battered school laptop in the passenger seat of Britta's car,

"*. . . he's passed on to That Big Jackpine in the Sky. And while this may be an uncharitable view to take of one of God's own creatures, I cannot say I'm sorry.*"

"That *is* uncharitable," I remarked to Britta. "The poor porcupine was just trying to get out of the cold. He didn't know he was in Mary's basement. I bet he figured it out when Mary started shooting at him."

I began to giggle. A lot. I couldn't stop.

Britta glanced at me from the driver's seat. She wasn't smiling. "Uh-huh."

"She says herself it was cold: 'Jack Frost's gnarled fingers . . .' Paul Marshall's diesel wouldn't even start. He and Lynn couldn't get to church. They had to listen to the sermon on the radio."

"June," Britta began. She didn't finish.

Poor Britta—how to express to the person sitting next to you in a moving vehicle that you were afraid she was going nuts?

I couldn't explain it: my strangely giddy, light-hearted mood. Getting in the car with Britta this morning, two days after my mother's memorial, had been the first thing that made me laugh and crackle with excitement since we found her dead.

"What?" I said.

"Hand me my sunglasses, would you?"

I got Britta's sunglasses out of the glove compartment. Then I pulled my own gargantuan movie-star shades out of my purse. All the clouds were breaking now and the sun in that sparkling blue sky was blinding on the new snow. It was painted heavily on the branches of the tall, dark green pines. On our left, blue-white patches of the frozen Pluie River glittered through breaks in the trees.

The world was bright and so lovely. I wanted to enjoy it. Just days before, I had thought I might never enjoy it again.

Visions of glorious days ahead were hurtling deliciously through my brain every time I closed my eyes. Parties in glamorous houses. Gardens with twinkling lights. The smell of heavy blossoms in the air. Wild and beautiful costumes and clothes.

Cake served on painted plates, each piece accompanied by a flower . . .

"I want a doughnut. Don't you?"

Britta sighed and clucked her tongue. She turned on the radio and listened to the news for a few seconds. Then she turned it off again.

"No," she said.

I sobered up a little and went back to typing Mary Dostal's coffee column. I moved on to Alvina Lund's news from Bagwajipin. For obvious reasons, I was skipping the School News column this week.

I finished and shut the laptop and stowed it in the backseat. I pulled Tonya's phone out of my pocket. A small, cheap-looking flip phone. Any texts that might have been sent or received over that line had been deleted. There were no photos or voicemails, either. I scrolled through the contact list.

"Bobby. C.J. Violet," I recited to Britta. "Do any of those sound familiar to you?"

"No . . ."

"Shelley P.? Stan Wabose?"

"No. June, I'm not sure about this."

"About calling these people?"

"You're not calling anyone, are you?"

"Not yet."

"Just wait, June. Let's think."

"Wait for what?"

"Should I be doing this with you?"

"I'm just making a list." I held up my gel pen and a piece of paper.

"I mean going to Duluth."

"Well," I said, eyeing her, "it's too late now."

"No, it's not." Britta glanced at a road coming up that turned off Highway 400. We weren't even yet at Vogel, where we'd hook up with 443.

"No. Britta. Please."

It had taken so much convincing to get her to go at all. I hated to have to start all over again. Especially when the last two days had been filled with nothing but arguments.

My mood had been so high just ten minutes before. Now, it plunged. I leaned back into my seat and hung my head. I wrapped my scarf around my neck so I could sink down into it up to my ears.

Then I cried. I was crying all the time now.

"June. June," Britta said. "Okay. All right."

"Don't turn around. Please, Britta."

"I won't. I'm not." She even sped up a little, to prove how much she meant it.

Still I kept sobbing. I couldn't stop. My scarf got soggy and covered in snot.

I thought back to the evening of the memorial, when I'd snarled at Aunt Sylvi. And not only Aunt Sylvi, but Zee, too. I'd be surprised if she ever wanted to talk to me again.

Then again, why should I care?

Care about Zee? My supposedly dearest and closest friend, who had, when I shared with her the earth-shattering news that my mother had once worked as a prostitute, grabbed me, held me tightly, and said—

"I know, June. I'm sorry."

We had been in Zee's car at the time, the rusty Cavalier she had bought with the $900 she made two summers before washing cars in her father's garage. She was about to drive me home from the memorial. We were waiting for the engine to warm up. We could see our breath in the air.

"What?" I pulled away from her. "How?"

"I mean—I should say I guessed . . ."

"Did Uncle Aaron tell you?"

"No—does he know?"

Finally, Zee told me the whole story. How, at that degenerate party in Canada last summer, the one I'd heard so much about, Frank *had* approached Zee to ask if she were interested in making a little money. But not by selling drugs.

"Are you *serious*? How could you not tell me that?"

"June, I wanted to. I thought sometimes that I should. Then, at other times, I thought—"

"You're sure that's what he meant? Frank?"

Which meant that he was involved, too. Which meant . . .

"Why do you think he asked *you*?"

My tone was vicious. Zee lowered her eyes and looked at her hands. She played with the hem of her black suit coat, sticking out from under her short leather jacket.

"I don't know," she muttered.

I knew. At school this fall, I'd been apprised of the sordid situation at that party by one of the nastiest souls in our grade:

Carter Nordlof. Who told me that I ought to know about the spectacle Zee had made of herself. Drunk and high, smoking cigarettes until she puked.

And, worst of all, throwing herself at nearly everyone at the party!

Boys, girls, even the adult men and women who were there. Touching their knees, stroking their necks, running her long, elegant fingers through their hair. Kissing anyone who would kiss her back. Moving on to the next drunk lap whenever anyone shoved her away.

They let it go on, said Carter Nordlorf, only because it was so hilarious . . .

"Jesus, Zee," I'd said when I confronted her about it, in September, "are you crazy? With those people?"

"Not all of them are so bad."

"You're lucky you didn't get killed."

"I don't care. I'm sick of being scared. Anyway, it was Spin-the-Bottle. Everyone was—"

"That's not what I heard."

"You believe that asshole over *me*?"

Why had Frank approached her? It wasn't hard to see.

"He saw you slutting out like that," I said to her now in her car, "and he figured—"

"Hey."

I was surprised at the sharpness in Zee's voice. I barreled ahead. It was *my* time to be mad.

"He figured—" I tried again.

"He was falling-over drunk, June. Otherwise, I don't think he would have said it."

"And Tonya—"

"No." Zee's tone was a little softer. "Your mom was mad when she saw him talking to me. She yelled at him. She even hit him. After that, they left . . ."

"Hit him?" Tenderhearted Tonya? She didn't even like to kill hornets when they got into the apartment through holes in the window screen.

"Just, like, swatted him . . . But she was mad. And she asked me what I was doing there. She asked if you were there."

"She was trying to find me?"

"I think she was afraid you'd see her."

I pictured this for a minute. Tonya shoving drunken Frank towards the door. Looking around furtively. For me.

"What did Frank say to you?"

Zee's lips curled. "He said there might be a market for me. Some people wanted something 'a little different' . . ."

"That's disgusting."

"Did I say it wasn't?"

"Well—" For some reason I couldn't stop myself—"what was he supposed to think, I guess. Seeing you stoned out of your mind—"

"Stop it."

"Slutting out with everybody in the freaking room—"

"Fuck you, June."

I stopped in shock. At first Zee looked surprised, too. Then she narrowed her brown eyes.

It was at least a minute before one of us spoke.

"My mother just died," I said, trembling.

"No," said Zee, shaking her head. "No. I know that. And I'm sorry. But you think that makes it all right? To slut-shame me? You have no idea. You have no idea what things have been like for me here. You think we're the same, but we're not. Things have always been easier for you. You think you're different like me. But you're just—normal."

"You think it was *normal* growing up with Tonya?"

"At least she accepted who you are."

"No, she didn't. She accepted who *you* are. It hasn't been easy for *me*, being around all you skinny people, either . . . I don't think you ever think of that . . ."

"Oh, come on," Zee snarled, "you're going to compare that to *this*?"

"I don't know why it has to be a contest . . ."

"You're the one who's making it that way . . . Listen, June. Sometimes I just have to relax. Forget about things. Drinking, you know, pot, whatever—it helps."

"I know more about it than you do. I know what it can do to you. Frank and Tonya—"

"People grow up," Zee said loudly. "People change. And you're going to have to accept it. Or else—"

"Or else what?"

Zee shrugged.

"You're the one," I said plaintively, "you're the one who always said we should wait . . . keep ourselves apart from all the slobs who couldn't . . . appreciate us . . . wait until we had other people around us who made it worth it . . ."

It was a beautiful and thrilling vision Zee had always painted for our future: the one with the flowers, the gardens, the poetry. The worthwhile affairs, the artful cocktails.

Certainly, I had never wanted to engage in any of that while I was still living with Tonya. I couldn't stand the thought of giving her the pleasure of hearing about it.

"It's about time, June!" she would have crowed.

"When we were kids, June," Zee said now. "I didn't feel like waiting anymore."

"You said it wasn't worth it. You said—"

"And now you're not going with me to the Cities, anyway. Are you?"

"You made a fool of yourself. All of them were laughing at you, you know."

"I know," Zee said. "So what? Not everyone can be a prude forever like you. At least I wasn't at home watching a Disney movie with my cat. And wishing my mommy would come home."

I gasped and started crying. "You think I care what you think? I could care less."

Through my tears, I saw Zee staring at me, unmoved. She put on her best starchy librarian expression.

"*Couldn't* care less," she said.

I got out of her car then. Before I slammed the door, I looked in. She was staring fiercely at the steering wheel.

"Just so you know," I said, "I talked to Carla today. She doesn't have any problem with you—except that she thinks you're a racist."

I started walking. A few seconds later, Zee peeled away up the street, the bald tires of the Cavalier spinning out on the ice.

When I was out on Highway 400, I felt a car slow down behind me. Aunt Sylvi and Uncle Rich, pulling up in their stately sedan.

I got in without saying a word. After a while, Aunt Sylvi asked if I were all right.

I shrugged. Uncle Rich, in his leather bomber hat with furry flaps, reached back and patted my knee. I squeezed his hand before giving it back.

I thought about what Aunt Sylvi had told me earlier. That when Tonya came to her, she said she wanted to keep her baby. Me. And being pregnant was the main reason she didn't want to keep "entertaining" at greasy parties in the woods or blowing strangers in Lisbeth motel rooms anymore.

But she needed help to get out of it. That was how she made most of her money. So Aunt Sylvi and Uncle Rich supported her until I was a little over three years old.

Aunt Sylvi said Tonya was a good mother. She had always been good with babies. Sweet and tender, pulling goofy faces. Strapping me into a backpack and taking me into the woods. Popping wild raspberries into my mouth.

But Aunt Sylvi could tell Tonya didn't like being dependent on them. She was proud. She wanted to take care of herself.

One day, she said she didn't need the money anymore. She was doing well on the handyman jobs and the furniture, she said.

Especially the furniture, which she could work on while I stacked blocks in a playpen. I was a docile, content baby. I never liked to stray far. I seemed to even like being penned in.

Certainly, Tonya said, I liked it better than being hauled into the woods, where I cried at all the flies, startled at every sound, and complained about the feel of pine needles under my tender little feet.

Aunt Sylvi kept sending checks, anyway. After a few months, Tonya started sending them back.

"Did she start doing it again?" I asked Aunt Sylvi now. "When she stopped taking the money?" I looked out the car window at Aulneau's dark, almost empty streets.

"She said she wasn't. But I don't know."

"Britta told me about some of the girls who get into this. She said it's not as uncommon as you'd think up here."

"Unfortunately, it's not. I used to work in social services in Binesi. Did you know that, June?"

I squinted. Someone had told me once, but I had forgotten. It was after Aunt Sylvi finished college. She moved back to northern Minnesota for a couple of years to work about two hours south of here, before settling in the Cities with Uncle Rich.

"Some of these girls don't know what else to do. There aren't many jobs in Binesi," Aunt Sylvi said.

"Did you ever think of moving here? After Tonya came to you? To look out for her?"

Aunt Sylvi hesitated. She glanced at Uncle Rich in the passenger seat. "Yes. We did think about it."

"Why didn't you?"

"Oh. Selfishness, I guess. We liked our home. Being where we were. Your Uncle Aaron liked it, too. He was happy in the city. We hated to uproot him again."

"And Tonya wouldn't move."

"No. She would have hated being away from the woods."

"She could have stayed at Otten's. Or found some other job."

"Yes."

"So why didn't she?" I cried. "How could she have liked—*that*—better?"

"You can't think there are many people who like it, June. People fall into things. Sometimes when they're young, being reckless . . . Or they're desperate for money. Or their parents sell them into it—all kinds of things happen. Then that's what they know. They don't have a work history of anything else."

"That's not what happened to Tonya. She had good parents."

"Who died when she was still young."

"So? Tonya didn't even like her parents."

"June." Aunt Sylvi sounded shocked. "That's not true. Where did you get that idea?"

"She never talked about them."

"It's not true . . . Tonya was a little wild. She liked to have fun. She liked to go to parties. She may not have liked her parents trying to stop her. Her mother and my brother maybe didn't quite understand Tonya. They were more—well, they were more like you, June. Homebodies. But they were all close in their own way."

I frowned. "She never told me."

"She was probably ashamed. If she talked about them, then she had to think about them. Then she had to think about how they would feel about what she was doing."

"Ashamed . . . Good . . . I hope she was ashamed . . ."

"June."

"Do you think it was Frank who got her into it? After they met at Otten's?"

"She never told me that. But that's what your Uncle Aaron thinks."

"She could have just kept working there," I said again.

"A factory job was hard for someone like Tonya. Doing the same thing every day, at the same time every day."

"That's ridiculous," I said viciously.

"And June—when she was in high school, something happened to Tonya."

We were at the apartment. Aunt Sylvi parked the car.

"What? What happened to her?" I asked her sharply. "You mean, like—she was raped?"

Aunt Sylvi sighed. It was in the winter. Tonya was at a party on the lake. She went with a few of her male friends from high school. They weren't able to stop—or didn't try to stop—a group of three men from assaulting her. One of them was a tourist who had come from the Cities to fish. Two were from a couple towns over. Tonya had never met them before. She said she never saw them again.

She didn't tell her parents. She only told Aunt Sylvi when she was trying to explain how she could have chosen to be a prostitute after going through something like that.

"She didn't want to be defined by being a victim," Aunt Sylvi told me. "And in some mixed-up way, it made sense for her to get into the business to achieve that. She said who and where and when. And she got something back for it. She said that gave her a feeling of control."

"Not be defined by it?" I said. "She defined her whole life by it."

"None of us can know what it's like, June, without having gone through that experience ourselves."

For a while, the three of us just sat there in the cooling car. Then it started to get really cold. Finally, Uncle Rich got out. He opened my door and held out his hand and stood there until I took it.

He hugged me and said, "People aren't just one thing, June."

Sure. Right. Was he talking about Tonya? Or was he talking about *me*?

I was—the daughter of a prostitute. The daughter of some *john*?

Tonya had never denied it, Aunt Sylvi had said. Or suggested there was any more likely possibility . . .

By the time we got into the apartment, I had worn myself out. I met Uncle Aaron's eyes but didn't speak to him. He watched me nervously as I walked around the room.

I pulled a journal I hadn't looked at yet off Tonya's shelf. I took it to my bed and leafed through it.

Nothing of substance, nothing at all . . . what did I expect? With a life like that, who wouldn't have skipped the gritty details in favor of scrawling abstract nonsense about rainbow gatherings and channeling the divine?

The entries didn't even seem to be in any particular order. There were hardly any dates at all. As a record of anything, they were worthless.

I let the book slip from my grasp and watched it go. It banged to the floor.

In mid-bite at her food dish, Enid startled and hissed. Uncle Aaron, sitting at the kitchen table, jumped, too.

He complained to Aunt Sylvi. "I wish you wouldn't have—"

"Shh." Aunt Sylvi eased herself onto Tonya's bed and laid her cane on the floor. She looked at Tonya's pillow and patted it. She kept her hand there for a long time.

"Not today. We're tired," she said.

I opened the plastic bag Jack had given me. There was almost nothing in Tonya's wallet except for a couple credit cards and seven dollars. Her library card and pressed sprigs from a cedar tree.

I scrolled through her phone. Jack was right. Nothing but texts to me, Ruby, Britta, a few other people, banal stuff. Making plans, finishing painting jobs. Solidifying an agreement to feed someone's horses while they were away.

I looked at her pictures. Wildflowers. Icicles hanging from

the eaves of a barn. A deer near a wire fence. A bright blue bird on the leafless branch of a tree.

There were very few people in any of them. No one I didn't know.

Not as many texts to Frank as I expected. That was the only surprising thing. He had said they checked in with one another every day.

I put the phone away, picked up the journal, and put it on my nightstand. I stood up with my hands on my hips and looked around the room.

I started digging. I opened the closet door and stuck my hand into the pockets of all of Tonya's coats. I ran my hand over the shelves in the back before I moved on to her dresser and started sifting through her underwear.

No one in the room dared asked why . . .

Uncle Rich had been sitting in the rocking chair, examining one of its creaky joints. He got up and started opening and closing the junk drawers in the kitchen. I watched him, his thick gray hair sticking up and staticky after taking off his leather hat. His khakis were rumpled but his striped dress shirt was still tucked in. He was humming faintly: "Bridge over Troubled Water."

At one point, he opened the refrigerator and pulled out one of the dark brown bottles of beer he had put in there. He offered Uncle Aaron one.

Uncle Aaron said testily, "I don't drink. You know that."

I rifled through Tonya's hand tools. She kept them on a stack of plastic shelves in one corner of the room. I found a cardboard box filled with screwdrivers and small brown paper bags of screws of all shapes and sizes. I brought the box to Uncle Rich in the kitchen area and set it down on the counter without a word.

Then I went back to my search. I found it on one of those tool shelves, the last place Tonya must have thought I would ever look. In a metal box, nestled beneath a pile of sandpaper.

I lifted the last rough sheet and smiled. I dropped it into the pocket of my cardigan: a cell phone I'd never seen before.

Before I put the box away, I saw a glimpse of light blue under another piece of sandpaper. I moved it aside. A flat plastic rectangular compact. I wasn't sure at that moment, but later, I confirmed it: birth-control pills.

I joined Uncle Rich in the kitchen. He was sorting screws in his palm. I leaned my head against his arm.

Then I straightened up, opened a cabinet, and took out a cup.

"You want some coffee, Uncle Aaron?" I said.

THIRTEEN

The following morning, I had gone out onto the sidewalk and called Britta.

"Do you still have those addresses?"

"Yes—why?"

I told her I was going to Duluth. I would go to those houses and talk to whoever was there.

Britta paused. "And say what?"

"Find out what they know? I've got pictures. Tonya. Tonya and Frank."

"June, to tell you the truth, I was planning to go myself. But I'm not taking you."

"Why? You think I'm too stupid? That I'll mess it up?"

"Because I promised Jack I wouldn't. I gave those addresses to him, too. And yes, June. You don't have a lot of experience with something like this. Frankly, you don't have *any*. So I'm going alone. Would you mind lending me those pictures, though?" Britta said.

"I've got pictures of Tonya and me together. So they can see I'm for real. That I just want to know what happened to my mother."

Britta was quiet.

"That could be useful," I said. "Right?"

"Hm," she said.

"I can't stay here right now. I have to go somewhere. Do something."

"When are you going back to school?"

I pictured it: being in school when Zee and I weren't speaking to each other. We had never had a fight that pulled us this far apart before.

And while everyone was whispering behind my back about my mother . . .

It was going to come out. Things like this always did. And what did other people already know? Secrets didn't stay secret for long in a small town like Aulneau. And this secret was an old one.

I was racking my brains. It was torture. Had anyone at school ever dropped some sly comment about my family that I was too naïve to understand?

I couldn't be sure they had, I couldn't be sure they hadn't. I was never going back to that school again.

I didn't want to go anywhere where anyone knew me. I wanted to get out of town. It was humiliating. What did it mean, to be the offspring of some anonymous sleazebag who paid for sex? What did that make *me*?

"I want to do this first. Come with me," I said to Britta.

"You're driving there?"

"Well." I told Britta the situation with Tonya's car.

"Ah," she said and sighed.

"Please. If you don't take me," I added, thinking fast, "I'll ask Frank."

"*Frank*? June, that is a bad idea. No."

"What choice do I have?"

"I bet he wouldn't even agree. If he's afraid of what you'll find out."

"Well. I guess I won't know until I try."

The next day, we were on the road. We made the trip, driving first east along the border, then south over the Iron Range, in just under four hours.

By that time, the lovely, floaty feeling I'd had at the beginning of the trip was long gone. An obliviousness that looked only into the future and didn't remember a past—a sensation that made me feel almost as if I weren't in my body at all.

My body didn't feel exactly like my own anymore. It looked the same. My long fingers. My thighs in my corduroys.

All my parts looked familiar. But familiar as if they belonged to someone I knew, or even just someone I saw regularly in two dimensions on TV.

As we came into the city, I tried to focus on it. I reminded myself of how much I liked Duluth. Multi-story houses slanted into the hills. The red-brick buildings downtown and the clock tower. The black-and-white lighthouse at Canal Park. The glorious Glensheen Mansion, built in 1905. In the 70s, a rich heiress had been brutally murdered there for an inheritance, just like in a story.

Lake Superior was frozen where it curved into the shore. Sheets and chunks of ice moved in the high waves farther out and massive iron-colored ships and freighters rested at the docks.

The neighborhood of the first address was up a steep hill from downtown. The streets were slippery.

We parked in front of a tan brick duplex next door to a vacant lot. A couple of trash bags and a ragged blue tarp were half-buried in snow. There were no other cars parked nearby.

Britta put on the parking brake. It was only then that I dropped the bomb on her: the news Aunt Sylvi had given me two days before.

"Wow. So it's for sure?" Britta said.

I stared at her. But I was so used to this scenario by now, I could hardly summon up any surprise.

"How long have you known?" I said.

"I didn't know. But I also didn't see how the work she did ever added up. Especially when Jack told me she had bought that land . . . These last few days, I've been asking around town about Frank, too."

"What about him?"

"Get this: his father used to run a brothel. Frank grew up in it. Some skeezy place out in the woods."

I told Britta about the birth-control pills. "And you're sure she didn't have a boyfriend?" she said.

"Did she ever talk about a boyfriend to *you*?"

"Oh, June. I think you'd better brace yourself."

I told her I was used to doing that by now. She took a notebook out of her pocket. I watched her.

"Are you writing a story about this?" I said.

"I run a newspaper, June."

"I don't mean for the *North Star Herald*. You're trying to get this in some big paper, aren't you? That's who you were talking to on the phone the other day."

"I won't use any names. I promise. But if this is connected to a bigger story, one that people need to know about—"

"Well, I would hope not." Names? I hadn't even thought of that. "Promise me you won't use my name, Britta."

"I just told you I wouldn't. But these things need to see the light of day. That's my job." Britta's bright blue eyes were blazing now. She put her hand on the door handle, then looked again at me. "Is there anything else I should know before we go?"

I thought for a minute, then told her what Zee had told me about Frank and the party in Canada. Britta nodded.

"Tonya never let on to me," she said. "She must have had to be so careful."

"Right. Who knew my mother was such a good liar."

Britta gave me a look of soft reproach. "Every word she said. Think about it . . . Well. I'm sure you can see why, June."

"She didn't want to go to jail?"

"She didn't want *you* to know. She knew you were already embarrassed of her."

"Embarrassed?" I winced. "Is that what she thought?"

"Well, weren't you?"

I began gathering up my materials. Tonya's burner phone, the manila envelope of photographs. My heart was racing a little.

"Can we just do this?" I said.

Outside, my scarf, still damp from my tears, immediately began to stiffen in the cold. When no one came to the door after we rang the bell, we started knocking. Nothing. We stood there knocking intermittently for several minutes.

Britta began to knock on the other door of the duplex. I said, "No, it's this one."

"If you want to know about someone, June, ask the neighbors."

No one opened the door there, either. The second address brought us to a white frame house only a few streets away. We climbed a set of icy steps that inclined sharply from the sidewalk.

I walked gingerly, holding onto the iron railing. Stupidly, I had worn a pair of silly little flats with no tread.

I heard a creak and looked up to see a woman slowly opening the door. She stayed half-hidden behind it.

But she didn't look small or scared. She was hefty and strong-looking. Middle-aged, with a flinty expression and a long gray ponytail.

Britta had already sprung up the steps and was on the short walk leading to the house. Her mittened hand up in greeting.

"Hi, there," she said.

She was turning on the charm. Using the sugary, childlike voice that tended to get her whatever she wanted.

The woman just looked at her. Then she flicked her light green eyes onto me.

"Hello!" I tried to wave and nearly fell. I felt like a roly-poly clown out there.

The woman didn't speak. She made me nervous. She reminded me of teachers or speech judges that I knew at first glance were going to be exacting and severe. The kind who with one stolid look could make me feel like a preeny and fluffy and superficial little ditz with my Cleopatra eye makeup and my prissy shoes and my "Creative Expression" speech peppered with jokes and puns.

Britta introduced both of us and said we were here about Tonya Bergeron. The woman's face didn't change.

"I'm her daughter," I said.

I offered up a smile. I hoped it looked composed, competent, and disarmingly pathetic all at once. It wilted when she didn't return the favor.

"We're looking for her. Have you seen her?" Britta said.

I glanced at her. The woman watched me sharply.

She said, "No one told me you'd be coming."

I struggled to keep myself from looking at Britta again. What now?

After a beat, Britta said, "Oh. Well—"

The woman took a step back. I came forward, clutching my envelope and pulling off my gloves.

"Please wait. See?"

The woman's blank expression didn't change but she stopped closing the door. She let me show her several photographs of Tonya and Frank. Then one of my mother and me together. The pictures were all still sticky on the back. This morning, I had pulled them off the posterboard we had put up for the memorial.

In the photograph of Tonya and me, we were standing behind a cake we had made for Uncle Aaron's birthday. I baked it, Tonya dotted the white frosting with orange sugar flowers. Her thin arm was wrapped around my neck and she was kissing my cheek. My eyes were lowered in embarrassment, but I looked happy, anyway.

Our bodies were different but our faces were much the same, even down to the light freckles on our noses.

"See?" I said again. I touched the picture, then my own face, as if the woman didn't speak English.

The woman looked at the photographs, then up at me. "I can't help you."

"You don't know her? She gave us this address."

"Are you Andrea, by chance?" Britta said.

The woman shot her a grim look. She took a tighter grip on the door. "No."

"C.J.?" I said. "Violet?"

"I need you to get off my property. If you don't, I'm going to come back out here with something you're not gonna like."

I put my head down and felt Britta take my elbow. She hurried me down the walk. I slipped and grabbed the railing to catch myself.

"It's okay. I've got you. Get to the car, June," Britta said.

Though when we got there, she took a moment to write down a note in her pad before starting the engine. I was trembling.

"Shouldn't we go?" I was staring at the house, waiting for the door to open and a gun barrel to appear.

"She didn't really mean it. She just wanted us to leave. It's not the first time someone's said something like that to me," Britta said.

I didn't relax until we were several blocks away. I felt a little sick, but my stomach growled. It was 12:30 and I hadn't had anything to eat since breakfast but a string cheese from the gas station.

"Lunch?" Britta said.

In a brew pub downtown, it was Britta's turn to be in a funny, high-spirited frame of mind. I slowly chewed my wild rice burger, feeling fairly subdued.

Britta took a drink of a tall beer that was almost black. With her two braids, her olive-green stocking hat, and her navy pea coat, she looked just right in the place. The exposed beams and rafters, the old-timey-looking bar. The beams plastered with concert posters and political stickers. The college student with the glasses, reading a thick novel. Sitting on a stool at the bar, his leg hanging down. Sipping a beer and underlining things.

I saw him take a look at me, too. That was nice.

Britta said brightly, "So. What did you notice, June?"

"What?"

"How did she threaten us? And how did she not?"

Apparently, Britta had decided that my apprenticeship was, in fact, in full swing. Now hardly seemed like the time.

"You mean how she seemed to want to shoot us?"

"And she *didn't* say she would call the police."

"Ah. Right."

"So there's probably something illegal here."

"Yes. I got that." I took a surly bite of a French fry. "You think that woman was, like, a madame?" It was hard to picture.

"Could be. Or—"

I watched her. "What?"

"I'm not sure yet."

"Do you think she knew Tonya?"

"Yes." Britta sat for a second and scratched the back of her head. The stray white-blond hairs at her temples were standing up in every direction. She reached for her hat, sitting between us on the table, and pulled it back on.

"You ready to go back to the first place?"

Before I could answer, an unfamiliar ring tone jangled out from my purse. I sat for a second before scrambling for Tonya's burner phone.

"It's 'Violet,'" I said.

Britta nodded and gestured violently. I answered "Hello?" and jumped up to move to a quiet corner in the hall that led to the bathrooms.

"Hello?" said a voice on the other end of the line.

It was a soft young female voice. I just sat there. I didn't know what to do. The girl did the same.

"Violet?" I said finally. "Hi. Can I talk to you?"

Only silence. I searched my mind wildly. Finally, I thought of something.

"Andrea?" I said.

The line went dead. Immediately I called back, but the girl didn't answer. The phone rang until it went to voicemail. No outgoing message. I didn't leave a message, either.

When I came back to the table, Britta was already standing up with her coat on. I told her what had happened and she stood there thinking for only a second before taking out her wallet and throwing way too many twenties on the table.

"This can't be a coincidence," she said.

On our way back to the white house, Britta asked me, "The person who answered the phone—could it have been the woman we talked to at the house?"

"No. This was a girl. My age, or—maybe younger. You think 'Violet' is Andrea?"

It had been a surprise to hear that young, high-pitched voice on the other end of the line. I don't know exactly who I had thought Andrea might be, but I had always assumed she was an adult.

We parked two houses away and put our eyes back on the white house. "Now what?" I said. "What are we looking for, exactly? Could Tonya have had another kid after me, you think?"

"I'm not sure how that would be possible. Wait, June—look."

I had already seen it—the door of the house opening. A girl came out. She was short and stocky and carried a big backpack on one shoulder. She kept her face lowered. Once on her way down the steps she paused and turned to look back at the house, before plodding the rest of the way down.

"Britta. I'm going to go talk to her."

"Go. I'll stay here in case we have to leave fast. If anything happens, run back to the car."

I was watching the door of the house closely when I got out. I left the passenger door open in case I had to dive behind it.

I crossed the street and began to walk towards the girl. She was coming my way on the sidewalk.

"Violet. Andrea. Please."

The girl walked a few more steps. Then she stopped and looked at me. I looked her over, too, searching for any resemblance to Tonya. I didn't see one. The girl was about sixteen. Her face was plump and round, her eyes small and dark. Her brown hair streaked with blond was tied into a bun on the top of her head. She had a big nose and small ears, already a little pink from the cold.

"Hi," I said.

Violet/Andrea stopped when we were about six feet apart and adjusted her pack. She watched me without speaking, with a kind of fatigued, placid impatience. She took one more step forward. She might have been hoping that, like a snake or a herd of cows, I could still possibly be spooked into backing up and getting out of her way.

I stayed where I was. After a minute, the girl turned with a little sigh and began to walk in the other direction. I followed, trotting on my slippery shoes down the icy sidewalk. Right past the white house with the tough gray-haired lady waiting somewhere inside, most likely with a rifle in her lap like a rancher under siege in the Wild West.

I caught up to the girl and walked beside her. "Violet. Or is it Andrea? It's Andrea, isn't it. I'm Tonya's daughter. You know Tonya? I have something to tell you." She was walking faster than I was. Her legs were short, but she was wearing better shoes. I had to catch my breath again before I could finish.

"She's dead," I said finally.

Andrea didn't stop walking; but she did slow down.

"I want to help you," I said.

Then I came up with: "My mother said that if anything ever happened to her, I was supposed to come find you and make sure you were all right."

Andrea did stop walking then. Slowly she turned to look at me. "Tonya's dead?"

Her voice was high and mild, almost sweet.

I nodded.

"How?"

"Shot. She was shot."

Andrea stared at me. An expression started to creep into her quiet eyes. She was afraid.

"Let's go somewhere. It's cold out here. We've got a car." I turned and pointed at Britta's red SUV still parked on the street. I waved even though I was now too far away to see if she were waving back.

"Who's that?"

"She's my friend. Tonya's friend, too."

Andrea shook her head. "No car."

"Right." I called Britta for advice. Andrea was now peering up and down the street. Britta suggested we meet at a coffee shop we had passed on the way here.

Andrea brightened a little. She said she knew the place.

The two of us walked there, more or less together, but in silence. I was out of questions for the time being. At least out of ways to phrase them.

The shop was pretty and light. It smelled like vanilla and toasted almonds and had yellow walls with paintings and photographs. At the counter, Andrea took off her industrial-looking black backpack, stuffed to the brim, and wedged it between her feet. With a faint anticipatory smile, she ordered the biggest sugarbomb coffee drink on the menu. I got one, too.

"To go," Andrea said.

When it was time to pay, she looked at me, and Britta stepped forward with her credit card.

Britta and I sat down. After hovering for a minute, Andrea sat with us, sliding her backpack under the table and resting her foot on it. She slurped up whipped cream and looked back and forth between us.

"Thank you for the coffee," she said in her melodious voice.

"Of course!" I cried.

"You're Tonya's daughter. Who are you?" she asked Britta.

"I'm a friend."

"She's my boss, too. At a newspaper."

Andrea took a long drink. There was whipped cream on her nose. She put down her paper cup. "Is that what this is about?"

"No," Britta said.

"I don't want to be in the paper."

"You won't be," I said. "We just want to help you."

"Okay. So what's the plan?"

Our lack of time to discuss in advance what to do when we had Andrea in front of us was beginning to show. I could feel it wearing on this awkward scene like a thin spot in my pants about to rip.

"Well," I threw out desperately, "what do you think? What do you need from us?"

Andrea turned slowly back to me and studied me for a long minute.

"You look like her," she said, "your mother."

"Yeah, but twice as big, right?" I tried to chuckle.

Andrea shrugged. "Are you like her, too?"

"How do you mean?"

I spoke brightly. But a shift in Andrea's tone had unnerved me. The lilt in her voice had gone flat. I felt my smile crack.

She clammed up then. She rolled in her small lips, gripped the arms of her chair, and pulled her head back a little so that her round face showed a double chin. She sank in her chair. I heard a faint scraping sound from under the table. She was pulling her bag out with her feet.

"What did Tonya tell you?" she said.

"She said—"

Britta interrupted me with a different tack.

"Nothing. She didn't tell us anything. The truth is, we're try-ing to find out what happened to Tonya. I'm sorry we didn't tell you right away, Andrea. But we can help you, too. Please trust us," she said.

Andrea was already standing up with her backpack on. She picked up her cup.

I said, "No, please—"

Then I grabbed her. She tried to shake me off. I held on tighter. "I need to know. I need to," I said.

Britta was hissing at me. I ignored her. On Andrea's face as she tried to twist her wrist out of my grip was not fear, but a determined, concentrated exertion. She looked not so much as if she were trying to escape from a tall, crazed teenager hulking over her, but methodically untie a knot or get a shovel into dry ground. Her tongue came out of her mouth a little.

Finally, Britta stood up to help. She grabbed my arm, the one that was holding Andrea. Then she smacked it repeatedly with her waspy little hand until I let go.

As Andrea booked it towards the door, I got up to go after her. Britta got a tight grip on my arm again.

"June! Can't you see how scared she is?" she said.

I glared at her. "She'll never call us back, we'll never find her again. How did you know my mother?" I called after Andrea.

I tried to get out of Britta's grip, but I couldn't. I was sur-prised at her strength. I guess she did paddle a lot of canoes.

Everyone in the shop was looking over at us. The girl behind the counter frowned down at the rag she was running over its stainless-steel top. Finally, Britta released me and I snatched my arm back and cradled it over my chest. I sat back down, my face hot.

"June," Britta said and groaned, "you really messed that up. I don't know what I was thinking, bringing you here . . ."

"Who is she? Do you think Tonya was helping her?"

Britta said in a low voice, "Helping her do what. That's the question."

"Get out of it—prostitution," I whispered. "Could that place we went to, that woman, be part of a safe house or something?" We had read about these places, sometimes unknown to the police, in the articles Britta had found.

"Or helping her get into it."

"No. She's just a kid," I said weakly.

Of course, that was stupid. If Frank had approached Zee . . .

For a while, we just sat there quietly, drinking. I felt exhausted. After she had downed her coffee, Britta went up and ordered a cup of herbal tea.

When she came back, I said, "What now?"

"Do you want to keep digging around? Or maybe we should just go home. I don't know."

"Dig around how? You mean look for Andrea?"

"No—well, maybe. I feel like, after all this attention we brought to her, she might be in danger now . . . So what should we do? I'm also thinking about the first house. The duplex. If you promise to keep your mouth shut and let me do all the talking."

I had already forgotten about it: the place where we hadn't gotten any answer when we knocked this morning.

I thought about it. Home did sound somewhat appealing, but only because I was tired. I wanted to sleep.

"Can we stay here tonight?" I said.

We went to a motel, ordered pizza, and turned on the TV. I ate so much I felt a little sick. Then I fell asleep at six-thirty and woke up at the witching hour.

Britta was asleep in the other bed. I went to the window and looked out onto the dark, empty street. Andrea was out there somewhere.

Doing what? Sleeping under a bridge? Why was she so alone that she had been willing to come with us, two strangers?

And what was she afraid of?

I thought about Tonya being in Duluth. Aunt Sylvi had told me that most of her work was arranged online. Maybe just to torture myself, I nonetheless pictured my skinny, shivering mother hauling herself up and down Duluth's frigid streets in a mini-skirt and high-heeled boots like in the movies.

For a few hours, I tried to fall back asleep. Finally, I turned the TV on and watched *Alfred Hitchcock Presents* at a low volume until Britta woke up at 8 o'clock.

A couple hours later, we were driving back to the neighborhood we'd been in the day before. There were two cars parked in front of the duplex today. But still no one came to either of the doors when we rang.

So we knocked at the house next door. A talkative woman in pajamas, probably about Tonya's age, seemed pleased to have company. From the smell of her breath, I realized that some of her good cheer may have been manufactured by an early-morning addition to her orange juice.

The woman pointed to a picture of Tonya and Frank. "I might've seen her. But I *know* I've seen him."

"Around here?" said Britta.

From the back of the house, a man said, "Who are you talking to?"

"Come meet Brandy and June. She's just looking for her mom." The woman smiled at me and I smiled back.

"Not here," she said. "At Archie's."

"And do you know where we could find Archie?" I asked politely.

The woman giggled. Britta said, "Archie's Bar?"

That's right, the woman said. And she'd seen Frank at a party in that neighborhood, too.

"Darla," the man called sharply, "who are they? You'd better shut up." I could see him, older than Darla, with a mean, pissy face, shuffling through the hallway and holding his back.

"You shut up," Darla called back to him.

Britta watched the man making his slow advance up the hall and asked in a hurry for the address of the house. Darla laughed. She didn't know shit about addresses. But she described the location, while Britta listened carefully.

Then Darla's smile disappeared. She looked at me sadly.

"But if she's there, you don't want to know it, honey. Okay?"

Darla's husband, or whoever he was, finally reached the door. He reached around Darla and pulled it shut.

"Don't fucking talk to people when you're drunk," we heard him say.

We drove to the west side of town. When we got out of the car, Britta looked uneasy. There was shouting coming from the one-story house we were about to walk up to.

We stood there listening a second. There was a small gray car in the driveway, and behind it a gleaming, massive pickup with oversized tires. Like something that was about to transform into a robot and ravage the town. I took a deep breath and went up the walk and punched the doorbell.

"June," Britta said behind me, "wait."

I faltered, looking back at her, but it was too late. A man, maybe in his late twenties, was opening the door.

At first, he looked like an ordinary kind of guy. Wearing a button-down shirt and jeans. His hair cut short and neat. Like a blond, older version of Jack.

He was good-looking. Nicely trimmed, wheat-colored facial hair, pretty blue eyes. Clear, smooth skin. I was fooled by that at first. I relaxed and thought I was in the presence of a regular person.

Then quickly I started to feel strange. Stiff and cold. His light eyes were looking at me as if I were a blank wall or a rock.

"What?" he said.

I stood and stared at him. He looked back at me. He flicked his eyes at Britta coming up behind me and began to look annoyed. He jutted his chin.

"Who the fuck are you?" he said.

I turned around and walked back to the car. As we were driving away, I dared to look back and then I wished I hadn't. The man was still in his doorway, watching us.

"Britta," I said when we were several blocks away, "I don't want to talk to anyone anymore."

"No. I think we shouldn't. Wow. I didn't like that at all. But just one more place, okay?" She was turning onto a street called Superior and parking. I looked out the window and saw we were at Archie's Bar.

I closed my eyes and shook my head. "I don't want to. Can't we just go home?"

"You probably can't go in, anyway. I'll just be a minute, June."

She grabbed my envelope with the photographs and went inside. I looked in the rearview mirror and locked all the doors.

The place had an aluminum front and a neon sign. Two places down was an old building that advertised the Rapids Hotel in faded blue letters on red-brown brick.

Britta took longer than I expected. I pulled out a book. Zee had given me *Anna Karenina*. She said it was just my thing, like a historical soap opera. I did like it, but it was hard to concentrate.

After a half hour, Britta emerged from the bar squinting at the sun. Before getting back into the car, she took out her phone and talked into it. I thought she was probably recording some notes. I had seen her do that before.

Thirty minutes earlier, I had been ready to turn my back on all of this forever. Now, I was curious again.

"Did you find out anything?" I asked her when she settled into the driver's seat.

"Let me figure out how to get out of town from here. I'll tell you when we're on the highway."

We'd been on 443 for about ten minutes and Britta hadn't volunteered any information. I prompted her.

"So?"

"A couple of people recognized Frank."

"What about Tonya?"

"Yes," Britta said slowly. "Tonya, too."

"And?"

"Well—they saw them there in the bar."

"Together? When?"

"Yes. Together. Um. A few times. In November."

"That would make sense. Tonya was gone for a while in November. Maybe she was staying around here doing something for the safe house?"

"It could be. Maybe."

"Maybe an undercover thing?"

Britta was quiet again as I watched her drive. She sat up very straight, keeping her hands primly at nine and three o'clock.

I said, "That's all you found out?"

"Yup. Pretty much."

"What about Andrea?"

Britta was quiet.

"Did you ask anyone if they'd seen Andrea?"

"June," Britta said. "Let me just—"

"What?"

"Let me think. Just let me think."

"What is it? Britta."

"People say things, but they don't always have firsthand knowledge. Until you confirm them, they're just rumors . . . Let me get home and make some calls and look some things up first."

For a minute, I was quiet and still. Then I reached out quickly for Britta's coat pocket. I tried to slip my hand in to get her phone. Britta slapped her hand down over mine and the car swerved. I felt the tires slip and I screamed.

I shrank back into my seat and gripped the edges and closed my eyes. Britta swore and someone honked.

Then the car was steady again. Britta swore a few more times. Her face was white.

"June. What is wrong with you? Don't you *ever* do that again."

I was frightened, too. I had never done anything like that. I did not feel like myself at all. I stared out the window at the flat road and fields and the ditches filled with snow. I began to cry.

"I just want to go home," I said.

FOURTEEN

We hardly spoke again on the drive. We got back into town around four.

Britta parked in front of my apartment and I turned to her. She looked straight ahead out the windshield.

I said, "What are you going to do now? Call Jack?"

"Jack, maybe some other people . . ."

"We could talk to him together."

"Jack and I need to figure out first how to—approach this."

"You mean how to tell me what you heard? Just tell me. I'm not a child, Britta."

Britta hesitated. She looked down into her lap.

"Could've fooled me," she said.

I got out of her car and left the door open so she'd have to shut it herself. When I got upstairs, I saw her plans were going to be foiled. Jack was waiting at the apartment door in his navy uniform.

"Britta texted me from Mink. You went to Duluth? What did you do, just start knocking on people's doors? Are you crazy?"

I unlocked the door and let him in. I turned on the lamp and looked for Enid. She was out of water, but had barely eaten a thing.

Jack took off his coat and hat. His collar and dark curls were damp with sweat. How long had he been waiting? He sat down in the rocking chair.

I took off my own coat and sat down on my bed. "Britta has to follow stories. That's her job."

"Not you. You're not getting paid for that. Britta was completely irresponsible."

"No. I made her take me. Have you talked to any of those people?"

"We were about to. You probably just made our job a lot harder. Well," Jack said and sighed, leaning back in the chair, which glided noiselessly now that Uncle Rich had fixed it, "you went to Duluth. So tell me what happened. Who did you talk to? What did you find? Anything important, you think?"

I just sat there smiling at him for a moment. I still felt odd. A little bit out of my body again, as I had been on the first part of the ride to Duluth. At the same time, very much in it.

"Come over here and I'll tell you," I said.

For an instant, the room seemed to turn a little. I felt dizzy, though not unpleasantly so.

Jack's phone rang. He pulled it out and silenced it. Then he put it back into his pocket and looked at me. Things came into focus again and I looked back at him, then around the room.

Four hours ago, this is where I'd wanted to be. Home. What about now? As far back as I could remember, every time I had climbed the stairs to this apartment and opened the door, after having been away, whether it was for a day or a week or an hour, I had stopped to listen for something before going in—a sigh.

I never heard it, not literally. Still, it was there.

A sigh of disappointment, of despair. A sigh that said, "There she is. Time to face my burden again."

I dreaded that feeling. Yet it didn't keep me away. It pulled me here, again and again.

If Tonya had wanted me around, I might have been ready to leave her . . .

Now, Jack—he was a different story. To Jack, I was a pleasure.

THE GIRL IN DULUTH

A joy. Every time I had seen him over the last few days, I had felt a little more sure of that.

He really was so attractive. His firm shoulders, his beautiful eyes. One long leg crossed over the other.

I knew it was time to stop and think. Instead, I just—didn't. It was as easy as that.

I had never even kissed anyone. In five minutes, that and a million other milestones had passed.

Jack pressed his face into my neck. I felt him pull some of my skin into his lips.

Then I was sliding out of my clothes. What a relief it was, like getting out of my skin!

Then Jack was not Jack. Jack was a tall length of—*flesh*. Tall and strong and moving and white. Very white, in a room with the lights still on. It was startling. I found myself wishing that both Jack and the room were a little darker.

More than anything, it was bizarre!

In a breathless voice, Jack kept asking if this or that was all right. I kept telling him to shut up. Being so mean felt luxurious. It sharpened my enjoyment of everything else.

He got on top of me and began to ask if—

"Yes," I said.

I was afraid it was going to hurt. It did. Then it didn't. Then it did again, but it was a fainter irritation that I knew was going to go away. Even in that moment, I could see beyond to the next time, and the next. Not necessarily with Jack.

Both of those types of aching grew and I wanted it to keep going even as, a few times, I almost pushed him off.

I knew how this was supposed to go. I could take it. I waited for him to finish.

Then I put my hands in his dark hair and kissed him.

"June. June!" He was covered in sweat now. There was no friction between our skin at all. He slid off, then buried his face in my chest.

For a few minutes, we were quiet, just breathing. That didn't last long.

At first, Jack said simply, "June. I'm so—glad."

Then: "I liked you for a long time. Even when we were still in school. Did you know that?"

I was less interested in answering this question, than in asking, "Why?" I was not disappointed in the answer, at first.

"You're beautiful," Jack said. "You're not like anybody else. When you dress like that, like you're in an old movie, it's so—" He closed his eyes and shook his head like a puppy getting out of the water.

I laughed and held his head between my palms again.

"What else?" I said.

Jack's handsome face took on a more thoughtful look. "You're not just sexy, June. You're smart. And serious about things. You know? Your head's screwed on straight. You seem, like—you can *do* things. Like: you could look at a house and know just how to set it up. So it works, so it's nice. You've even done that with this place. Look at that little teapot you've got there. You're so cute, June!" He kissed me and I kissed him back. "Imagine what you could do with a whole house. Wouldn't you like that? I can just see it. I guess, with everything you've had to deal with, you've had to grow up. Maybe faster than other girls. You always seemed—older, even than girls my age."

I tried to keep my smile intact. As he spoke, it was getting harder to hold onto it.

"Older?" I said.

"Like: ready to be an adult. Ready for . . ." Jack's eyes had a hopeful tenderness that couldn't be mistaken for anything else.

I didn't say anything. I kept stroking his hair.

"I want to take care of you, June," Jack said. "Can I tell you something? When your mom died, I got a little scared. I knew there was nothing keeping you here now. Because the rest of your family is already gone. And I know Zee doesn't like me.

THE GIRL IN DULUTH

She's been trying to get you away from here. Away from me."

"She likes you," I lied. "It's just—" I stopped, thinking of the first thing he had said. Yes. He was right. My family went back four generations in Tree Lake County. Even further back than that in southern Ontario. But in the last three generations, all of the branches had scattered.

"I guess that's true. I'm the last one. Aren't I," I said.

"And so am I. Unless . . . ," said Jack.

I looked at him for a moment more. Then I began to cry.

It was as it had been in the car with Britta—I couldn't stop. The sadness was so overwhelming, I couldn't pinpoint exactly where it was coming from. It was coming from everywhere, like rain in the wind. It was Zee, Uncle Aaron, Britta. Of course, it was my mother.

"Shit. Shit. June?"

Most acutely, there was a sharp terror wiring its way through my heart. We hadn't used any protection.

Perhaps a tiny, impulsive part of me had been thinking, 'Just get pregnant. Why not?'

If I did, then there was a clear path ahead. All uncertainty about my future gone. A simple, elegant solution.

Now, there was no going back. I turned onto my side towards the wall and curled up like a baby. I cried and cried.

Jack clutched my shoulder. "June. I'm so sorry. Maybe we shouldn't have—what's the matter?"

"Please just go."

"Are you kidding me? I can't leave you like this."

"Get out of here!" I was screaming now.

Slowly, Jack took his hand away. The spot where his sweaty hand had been was suddenly cold. I shivered. His side of the mattress lifted.

I heard the jangle of his belt and buttons. Then his hand was in the middle of my back.

"Don't." I shook him off, my face still buried in the pillow.

"June. I'm sorry. Maybe this wasn't—entirely appropriate."

I breathed in and out a few times. The pillow smelled of his cologne.

My voice was bitchy and I laughed. "Oh—you think?"

"Jesus, June, I'm a cop . . . You're still in high school . . . We should have waited . . ."

I was quiet then. I hardly breathed. Jack just kept standing there.

"Are you going to tell anyone?" he asked quietly, after a while.

I started to breathe again. "No."

Jack sounded hopeful. "Okay. But you should—if you feel like you need to."

"Okay."

"I can take responsibility for this."

I had my crying under control by now. I sniffed and wiped my nose. "All right."

Jack didn't speak for a few minutes. I heard him putting his coat on. "Do you really want me to leave?"

"Yes."

"Your uncle told me he went back to the Cities yesterday."

I groaned. "Please don't talk about him right now."

"I just want to—he's coming back in a few days, right?"

"Yes."

"And then what?"

"Jack."

"Right. Of course. We can talk about it later. June. I really don't want to leave you alone."

"I'm fine."

"Can I call somebody? Zee?"

"No. Please."

"And you're sure you don't want me to stay?"

"I am."

"What?"

"Yes."

"'Yes,' you want me to go, or—"

"I want to be by myself."

Finally, he was gone. Then I was mad he hadn't kissed me goodbye, and started crying again.

At some point, I fell asleep. I woke to a sound at the door.

Jesus, Jack! The guy couldn't leave well enough alone . . .

Only half awake, I turned onto my back. It was dark outside, but the lamp was still on.

There was a soft knock and the sound of metal jingling. Jack's holster and belt? I touched my chest and listened.

If I were being completely honest, I kind of wanted to do it again . . .

Then I heard a voice and seized up. I yanked the blanket up to my chin.

"June?"

It was Frank. I sat up, still covering myself, and peered across the room at the tab lock on the doorknob. It wasn't locked. Of course it wasn't. I hadn't gotten up and locked it after Jack left.

"Frank?"

"Juney?"

"Please don't come in."

Frank was quiet for a second. Then there was another brassy jingling sound, and the rattle of a paper bag.

"I came to fix the door."

"Oh . . ."

"Did you get my messages?"

I looked at the floor, where my coat was lying with my phone in the pocket. Apparently, I hadn't heard it go off while I was—preoccupied.

"Now's not the best time, Frank."

For a moment, Frank stood in silence. My heart was racing. Was I just stricken with horror at the idea of Frank coming in and seeing me naked in my childhood bed, with the sheets and pillows all in disarray and the room smelling of sex and sweat?

Or was it something else? I heard a shuffle of his boots. I looked at the shadows of his feet at the bottom of the door.

Frank said, "You know what. Jack called me. He wants me to come back to the station."

After a moment I said, "Oh, yeah?"

"Did he call you, too?"

I breathed in and out a few times. I tried to think quickly. "Yes."

"You know what it's about?"

"I'm sure it's nothing."

"Can I come in? I want to talk to you about a few things."

"About what?"

"I'd rather tell you inside."

Our apartment was the only one in the building. But I knew that downstairs, the feed store was open until seven. The clock on Tonya's nightstand said it was only six-thirty. Voices of customers sometimes carried up the stairs. I'm sure Sandy Levasseur heard her fair share of everything that went on up here, too.

Oh, God. Had she and her customers heard me and *Jack*?

"Why?" I asked Frank.

"It's no one else's business. I've got everything for the door."

"Later, Frank . . ."

"What is it?"

"What?"

"Are you afraid of me, Juney?"

There was a sorrowful note in his voice. I heard the paper bag of hardware scratch against the wood of the door. Was he leaning his head on it? Trying to see through a crack?

I thought of the house we had been to this morning. The blank, cold look of the man inside.

"Yes," I said softly, but loud enough for Frank to hear.

As soon as I heard his boots on the steps, I ran to the door in all my naked glory and locked it. Even though I was pretty sure Frank had a key, anyway. Tonya had given him one years before for emergencies. I couldn't think of any reason she ever would have asked for it back. I had never known him to use it, though.

I put on my thickest, most matronly pajamas and my bathrobe over that. Then I went to the bathroom. There was a little blood in the toilet and on the tissue. I was still aching down there.

In the mirror, I saw that while my rash was essentially gone, Jack, that vampire, had left a dark red hickey on my neck, not far below my chin.

I made my bed, then unmade it and changed the sheets. I sat on the bedspread, a little hot in all my layers, looking at my phone. Would Frank come back tonight? If someone else was here, he wouldn't want to come in.

I texted Zee. *I'm so sorry about everything. Can we talk?*

I smiled when she texted back only a few minutes later. *I'm sorry, too. Call 10 min?*

Can you come over? I said.

She texted back a thumbs-up. I remembered my problem and hurried to my dresser to find a turtleneck. But I couldn't wear it with my flannel pajama pants . . . I was still struggling back into my corduroys when Zee knocked at the door.

I opened it. Then I didn't know quite what to do. Zee looked as if she were feeling the same way. We had already apologized. We didn't hug right away, and then it was too late. Zee smiled shyly and came in.

"So," she said, laughing awkwardly as she sat down on Tonya's bed. She pulled Enid into her lap.

I went to the stove to make tea. Glancing over at her, I laughed awkwardly, too. But something about seeing her here, in this room where something momentous had just happened to me, made me feel more confident.

For years, Zee had been ahead of me in everything. Reading

and writing, math and music. She knew all about politics and history and social issues. And in the past year, she had learned things like: how to smoke a cigarette, and how to smoke a joint, and the difference between the two. She knew what it was like to be drunk. She knew how to drink so that you didn't puke, and how to drink when you didn't care if you puked or not.

I could have been doing those things as well. Zee had always invited me. But I was scared. Not only of what they might do to me, but of being like my mother.

For over a year, Zee had known what to do when someone else's tongue was in your mouth. She had first tasted that fruit one Saturday afternoon at an out-of-town speech contest. In a bathroom in the Charlette school, during that golden inter-school flirting hour between competition and the awards cer-emony, when the judges were tallying the points.

Well. Now I knew, too!

And I was 99.9% positive that for all her fooling around, Zee hadn't gone all the way with anyone.

I knew her secret: she wanted to. But she was apprehensive about the moment when she would take off her clothes.

Because then what would her partner see? Zee? Or just a girl, like every other girl? And was she a girl and only a girl? She didn't know for sure.

I knew her secret fears and uncertainties. As far as I knew, no one else did. Now, I had a secret, too.

I felt a smug little gladness as I gave my friend a cup of tea and said, "Guess what I'm doing tonight?"

Curled up with Zee on the bed, half-watching a DVD of a *Miss Fisher* that we'd seen several times before, and which was past due at the public library, I filled in a few more sections of my Common App for college. I even opened my school laptop and went to the site and created a username and password. I wrote them down neatly in my notebook.

At one point during the show, Zee sighed and looked at

me. She smiled. "Aren't you tired of this show yet? It's kind of bullshit, don't you think?"

"Why?"

"Well, it makes the police look like heroes and everything. You know they're always killing Black and Native people, right?"

"I know that. But it's not supposed to be a documentary. And that's in the U.S., too. This show is set in Australia, if you hadn't noticed."

"You think Indigenous people don't get shot by the police in Australia?"

"I don't know." I ventured, "But I bet you don't, either."

Zee frowned. Then she laughed a little. "That's true, I guess." She watched me type for a minute. "I'm so glad you're doing this, June. What would you do if you stayed here in town? Marry Jack and have ten thousand kids?"

I cringed. "Jack? I wouldn't marry *Jack*. Why would you think that?"

"I'm just saying—"

"Don't start," I warned her.

I put my laptop aside, crossed my arms, and tried to concentrate on the show for a while.

Then I felt something—a warm trickle, then a bigger gush, in my underwear. I went to the bathroom and pulled the yellow curtain as tightly closed as I could.

I sat on the toilet for a while until it stopped. Then I took a shower.

When I came out of the bathroom, I made a big show of yawning and saying how tired I was. I tried not to look as if I were holding the collar of my bathrobe over my neck.

I got under the covers of my bed as quickly as I could. Zee got off Tonya's bed and stretched and began to put on her coat.

I sat up, while keeping my chin down. "You're not leaving, are you?"

"I'm just going outside for a minute."

"To do what?"

"You know what. Don't start, June," she mimicked me. She gestured to my laptop, still on Tonya's bed where I'd left it. "You'd better get back to that. You've only got a little more than a week, you know."

"If you don't quit smoking, you're going to end up like Frank."

Zee flicked me off and went out the door. As soon as she was gone, I jumped up and ran to Tonya's bed and grabbed the laptop. Quickly, I went to the site for the Aulneau clinic. I made an appointment for the first available time the next morning. I finished and closed the tab just as I heard the creak of the street-level door downstairs.

That night, I slept with my phone on the pillow next to me. I'd turned the ringer down low. When my alarm went off the next morning, I got up quietly and slipped out of the apartment and closed the door right as Zee's alarm started to go off. I was turning into a good little sneak.

FIFTEEN

The morning was cloudy and warm, almost thirty degrees. I couldn't enjoy it. I was not looking forward to this.

On the way to the clinic, I passed Frank's house on the southern end of Central. It was a small one-story, with a fairly new coat of green paint he'd applied himself. A yard with a pine tree. His truck wasn't in the driveway. Was he at the police station, talking to Jack?

What had Britta heard about Frank and Tonya in Archie's Bar? From the way she was acting, it wasn't anything heroic and good.

I thought about Andrea. I had guessed she was sixteen. She might be even younger.

At the clinic, I was the only person in the waiting room. Thank God. And I didn't know the woman at the desk. She looked young, but she hadn't graduated from here. I handed her my medical assistance card.

"You're here to see Dr. Hedin?"

I shrugged and tried to smile. There were only two doctors to choose from, both men, one old and one not as old. The younger one was the father of the girl I stood by in choir, so I'd gone with the old one.

I was measured and weighed but no one told me to take off my clothes. I didn't know what to expect.

Dr. Hedin was at least in his seventies, maybe even eighty.

He was slow and small and he had a kind smile. I'd seen him around town before.

"So you're looking for some emergency contraception, June?" He asked me a lot of questions about sexual assault and feeling safe at home that I'd already answered on a stack of forms. I'd also recited my answers to the nurse who took my blood pressure and temperature. I guess they wanted to be sure.

Then he said, "Did you know you don't need a prescription to get the morning-after pill? You can buy it over the counter at the pharmacy."

"No." I stared at him. "You mean I didn't even have to come in here?"

"It's good you did, though, June."

He told me that the morning-after pill was less effective for women who weighed more than a hundred sixty-five pounds. According to the scale in the hall, I was two hundred and seven.

"What? I never heard that."

"For women over one-sixty-five, we recommend . . ."

Dr. Hedin described a medieval-sounding procedure involving a piece of copper and my uterus. I started squirming in my chair just thinking about it.

"No, no," I said, "I don't want that. There's a chance the pill might work. Right?"

"A chance—not as strong of a chance."

"Would I have to do it now? The procedure?"

"We could do it right now. That's what I'd recommend. The sooner, the better. In any case, within a couple days."

"But I don't want to. I'm only a few pounds over," I said.

"My recommendation is the IUD, June."

I was already standing up and thanking him. If earlier was better, and I was already at a disadvantage, then it was time I started hoofing it to the pharmacy.

As soon as I was outside the clinic, I suspected I was being stupid. Was it really time to be squeamish, when so much was at stake? Was I going to regret this moment later?

But I didn't want to turn around and go back in. I couldn't. I longed for Zee. I suspected she would have made me go. With her arm in mine, I could have done it.

I took out my phone and called her. She didn't answer. It was almost nine and she must be at school by now.

I stood there for a moment on the sidewalk. I wondered if Dr. Hedin and the nurse at the front desk were watching me from inside.

Finally, I decided I would go to the pharmacy and get the pill and take it. Then I'd go home, and this afternoon I'd tell Zee and ask her if she thought I should get the IUD, too. Maybe I could tell her I'd had sex, without revealing that it was with Jack?

I could imagine how that would go . . .

But if I told her it was Jack—

She would certainly agree with Jack that our encounter hadn't been "entirely appropriate." She might call it something worse than that.

Would she tell someone? Would Jack lose his job? I didn't know how all that worked when a girl was eighteen, but still in school.

Was I even still in school? I hadn't been near the building in over a week. I'd ignored every email I'd gotten from my teachers and the principal.

Frank still wasn't home, or at least his truck wasn't there. A gray car was parked in front of the house on the street. The engine wasn't running, but I could hear club music playing inside. It was the only car on the block. It looked familiar and I couldn't remember where I had seen it until I passed by and peeked in the passenger window. A man wearing sunglasses was sitting in the driver's seat. He turned and saw me, too.

Quickly, I looked away. I tried not to speed up. As I passed the front bumper, I put my head down and angled it just a bit so I could see the first part of the license plate: LPT.

It was the blond man from Duluth. The spooky one. I was sure of it.

I kept walking. I tried not to look as if I were in a hurry and mouthed the letters to myself. There was no one else on the street; this was the quiet end that was mostly houses. I wouldn't be in the business district for another few blocks.

I told myself I was sure he hadn't recognized me. I'd only glanced at him. And even yesterday, how long had he seen my face? Only a minute or two.

What was he doing at Frank's? Could it be a coincidence he was here today, right after I'd been in Duluth for the last two days, running my mouth about Tonya Bergeron?

Telling everyone my name and exactly who I was?

Maybe this guy just came to town to see Frank regularly? Stopped in to talk business or something?

I listened behind me. For several minutes, there was nothing. It was a quiet morning. A few birds in the trees.

Then there was an engine. I held my breath until the vehicle passed. I let it out. It was a blue car.

When I got close enough to see the shops up ahead, and a few people on the sidewalk, I began to walk faster. I ran across the street. When I got to the drug store, I finally dared to look at the street behind me. No gray car. No blond man on foot, either.

"LPT," I whispered, as I walked into the store.

The first thing I did was look in my purse for a piece of paper. But I didn't have a pen. I had to ask the woman at the front counter for one. She was standing there in her green smock surrounded by shiny red foil hearts and brightly colored boxes of children's valentines.

I knew her by sight, but I didn't know her name. She knew who I was.

"I'm so sorry about your mom, June," she said.

I gave her a trembling smile in return, then wrote down the license-plate letters and tucked the paper in my purse. How in the world was I going to buy the morning-after pill from this woman?

For a wild moment, I thought of stealing it . . .

I had to find it first. I headed to the back of the store past the batteries and the romance novels, where the pharmacy and health products were. There were no morning-after pills in the family-planning aisle. I went over every shelf twice, grimacing every time I saw the face of a smiling baby on a pregnancy test.

I checked the feminine-hygiene aisle. No luck.

Dr. Hedin had lied to me! Had he planned this all along, to force me to come back and get the IUD? I was in such a panic, this seemed perfectly logical.

Finally, I went to the pharmacy counter and asked, as quietly as I could. A middle-aged man was working there who I didn't recognize. Lo and behold, he had morning-after pills behind the counter. Apparently, they planned ahead for the devious intentions of shame-filled teenagers like me.

He handed it to me with a dispassionate expression. Best of all, miracle of miracles—"Would you like me to ring that up here?"

I could have kissed him. I thanked him profusely. I didn't even cringe at the price: a whole week's paycheck from the *North Star Herald*. He handed me a plastic bag with a courteous smile.

Then—oh, I was getting bold now—I asked, "Is there a bathroom here that I could use?"

I knew the store didn't have a public bathroom. For the first time, the man's eyes betrayed an emotion: a gleam of sympathy.

"Sure," he said, and let me behind the counter.

Locked into the bathroom, I took out the blue box and looked at it. The instructions said to take the pill with food to prevent nausea. They also warned that if you vomited within two hours of taking the pill, it probably wouldn't work. So you would have to take another one.

My stomach was sometimes unsteady even when I wasn't pumping it full of a big dose of hormones. I dug through my purse and found half a granola bar that had come out of the wrapper. I took a bite and almost broke my teeth. I held the stale granola in my mouth and sucked it until it was soft enough to chew.

My hands were sweating and it was hard to open the box. Once I'd triumphed over the packaging, I didn't waste a second. I popped the small white pill into my mouth and swallowed it.

There. I closed my eyes and breathed.

Now what?

Now, my other problem . . .

I couldn't stay in the bathroom for long thinking about it. The thought of the pharmacist coming to knock softly on the door to ask if I were all right was too horrid to contemplate.

I came out slowly and meandered to the front of the store. Thankfully, there were only a few people in the aisles. I entered an empty one, and, keeping myself as much as possible behind an endcap display, looked out the front window onto the street.

No gray car. No strange man. I gave the woman at the counter a hurried goodbye and took the plunge.

As soon as the mild air hit my face and I was walking purposefully along the sidewalk again, I began to feel a little better.

Why? Well. It was true that everything was a mess. In the last week, my whole life had fallen apart.

But, in the midst of all that, I had done something I was scared to do. I had gotten myself into a bad fix; but I had done something about it. I had made an appointment at the doctor and gone there alone. I had never even been to the doctor except for shots when I was little.

I had talked to a pharmacist, in public, about a truly embarrassing thing, like the eighteen-year-old adult I was.

I was proud of myself. As I started onto the bridge over the bay, I began to work up an appetite. I was looking forward to getting home and making a sandwich. Maybe a cup of hot chocolate, too.

I walked on the side of the street opposite to our apartment, just in case. As I got close, I looked carefully at the building and at everything around it.

There wasn't much to see. There was a pickup with a black tarp stretched over the bed parked in front of the feed store. As I watched, a man came out of the store and put a sack of something under the tarp and secured it and drove away.

Zee's car was gone. I had expected that. But I couldn't help but feel let down. I had hoped that maybe she would skip school to spend the day with me.

I scanned my eyes over the streets around my building. If the man from Duluth knew where Frank's house was, did he know where Tonya lived, too?

I saw the gray car coming up a side street and froze.

I ducked behind a parked car on Highway 400. Then I peeked around the bumper. As I watched, the blond man parked on the side street and got out. He went to my door and knocked on it.

Then he tried the knob. As he pulled open the door and disappeared up the stairs, my stomach turned and I almost cried out.

I pulled out my phone and called Zee. For a wild moment, I imagined her roaring up in the Cavalier, leaning over to throw open the passenger-side door. Tearing away in a spray of slush and flicking off the psychotic madman behind us, who was waving his fists in the air.

No answer. It was five minutes to ten o'clock. Undoubtedly, she was in physics right now.

I called Jack. I thought I had hit the wrong contact in my phone when Britta answered.

"June? I'm with Jack."

"What? Where?"

"In the car. June? What's the matter? Are you all right?"

"No." I told her what was happening. As I spoke, Britta began repeating everything I was saying out loud. I could hear Jack making muffled responses in the background.

"June, stay where you are. Jack's calling the station. Someone's coming for you. Randy? Maybe Nolan. We just left Duluth about twenty minutes ago."

"What?" I cried. "You're not here?"

"June, Andrea's dead," Britta said.

She told me that the night before, a girl in Duluth had been shot down in the street. Britta had left with Jack before the sun was even up to see if it was her.

"It was," she said in a low voice.

I felt stunned. Then terror and nausea started to creep back in. "You're sure?"

"Yes. June, where is he now?"

The man had been up at the apartment for several minutes. Had he broken in?

"LPT," I said instead of answering.

"What?"

"The license plate!"

The man came back out. He shut the door behind him.

I gasped. "Britta, where's Randy?" The man was on the sidewalk now. "He's coming."

"Randy?"

"No!"

I had been listening hard for a siren. Nothing. Were all the cops in another part of the enormous county? There were only four, including Jack.

I couldn't wait behind this car anymore. The blond man hadn't gone back to his car; instead, he was getting ready to cross the street.

Had he seen me? He wasn't looking exactly in my direction. Maybe he wasn't coming for me at all?

Or maybe he was pretending . . .

There was a gas station two blocks down. Maybe he was going there. But if he crossed the street and came up on the sidewalk at the spot he was heading for, he would see me hiding here.

If a semi hadn't been coming east on 400, I would have been screwed. It came chugging up from the main part of town, blasting out clouds of cold gray smoke. I saw the blond man make his calculation. Could he make it? The street was wide and there were patches of slush and ice.

He decided to wait, and I ran.

I went straight south through the neighborhoods for a few blocks. When I got to a big tree on a corner, I crouched behind it and held my breath as long as I could to keep from vomiting. I looked behind me. No gray car.

When I had calmed my stomach, I walked up to the house of the yard I was in and knocked. No answer. I knocked next door, looking up the street every few seconds.

Everyone must be at work. Weren't there any old people around here? I knocked on another door.

Ms. Karbo lived somewhere around here. But she was at school, two miles away.

I went back to the oak tree and leaned against it. Keep knocking on doors? Head back to the main part of town and get inside a store?

What if he found me when I was stuck on the bridge? What if he had a gun? Was he the one who had killed Andrea?

Gunned down in the middle of the street . . .

No sirens! I took out my phone again. There were texts from Jack's phone. Instead of looking at them, I called Frank. He answered on the fourth ring.

"I need help. Can you come get me?" I said.

"What is it? Where are you? The problem is, Juney—"

"I need help *now*. Frank!" I explained to him where I was. "I'll tell you why when you get here."

Frank groaned. "Juney, what's the matter? The only problem is, I'm in some trouble—I gotta lay low right now. I just got out of the shower, too."

"I know. He's here."

"What?"

"Someone killed Andrea," I said.

Frank didn't speak. I held the phone to my ear for a while. Finally, I realized he had hung up.

I leaned against the tree. It was good and solid. The scratch of the bark felt sort of nice against my cheek. My feet began to feel cold in my boots. I texted the numbers of the streets I was on to both Britta and Jack.

Where's Randy???? I typed.

Ten minutes passed. Fifteen. Finally, I heard sirens.

Britta called me, but I didn't answer. I straightened up. A vehicle was coming.

SIXTEEN

Frank was in a car instead of his truck. It was silver, and at first, I began to run.

Then he honked and called to me out the window. I turned around and got in.

One of the sirens sounded close, up on 400, maybe. The other one was coming into town from the west. Frank looked in the rearview mirror.

I sighed. After being out in the open, the little car felt as safe as a tank. It smelled of cigarettes and musky perfume. A string of pink beads hung from the rearview mirror.

"Isn't this Ruby's car? Where's your truck?"

"She's hiding it for me."

"Go to the police station, okay?"

Frank nodded and began to drive. He turned left at the next block, heading in the station's direction.

"Go faster." I looked behind us at the empty street.

"It's okay. They've got him."

Frank looked tired and somber, though less anxious than he had sounded on the phone. His gray-brown hair was wet and combed back.

"What?"

"They stopped him on 400."

"You saw him? The guy with the gray car?"

"Yeah."

170

"Who is he?"

"Oh," Frank said and sighed. He was still driving slowly east, possibly even slower than before.

"I saw him yesterday," I said. "In Duluth."

"I know. That was dangerous, Juney."

"At a house you'd been to before. How did you know?"

Frank looked into the rearview mirror again. He made another left.

"You weren't quiet about it. I was getting calls all day," he said.

"From who? What did they say?"

"Someone saw Andrea, too . . . I guess the last anyone knew she was supposed to be in Thunder Bay."

"Warning you about that guy—the blond guy?"

"Him. Some others, too."

"So how did you know him? Are you going to tell me?"

"Yeah," Frank said.

We were on the road that went past the station. Instead of turning in to the lot, Frank sped up and headed towards 400. At the junction, he glanced to the west, where we could see flashing lights of the squad cars stopped on the road. Frank turned east.

"Frank, what are you doing?"

"I want to tell you how it happened."

"Tell me at the police station!"

"They won't let me. You know that. They'll take me away before I can talk to you," he said.

He began to speed up. He was heading out of town.

I was scared at first. Then I gave up, and wasn't. It was almost as if I couldn't summon the energy. I was tired of being afraid.

I checked the time on my phone. If I could keep from getting riled up and barfing for just another hour—

"I wouldn't ever hurt you, Juney," Frank said.

I texted Jack. "Jack knows where I am. He'll send someone to find me."

"That's all right," Frank said.

He sped up again, so suddenly that I gasped. Ruby's car shook as he jammed it into fifth.

"Frank!"

He slowed down soon enough, after only a few miles. When we came up on Hartnell Rapids, Frank turned in and parked the little car as gently and quietly as an owl landing in a tree.

We stayed in the car. The snow on the rocks looked soft and wet under the clouds. A hawk was coasting in the sky. Once Frank started talking, he didn't stop.

He told the story of how he and Tonya had met at Otten's. How they became friends right away. Bonded. Two orphans.

Both of them hated the job. They bonded over that, too. Neither of them was made for working at a factory. Being on someone else's schedule. Being inside all day, making the same thing every day, so that rich people could get richer—

"I know all this," I said wearily.

They wanted to work when they felt like it and take a day off and go fishing when they felt like it, Frank continued, unperturbed. They wanted to make a lot of money sometimes. Then not work at all for a while if they didn't want to.

They wanted their freedom. Especially Tonya. That's why this appealed to them.

"*Appealed* to her? She was messed up from what happened to her when she was in high school. And you were, too!"

Frank looked at me.

"Because of your dad and what he did for a living. I know about that. I'm sorry, Frank. That must have been hard," I said, more subdued.

Frank shrugged. "I know what people say about my family. I know I'm supposed to think it was bad. But I don't know if it was or if it wasn't. I miss my father. I loved him and he was good to me. He was more of a man than I'll ever be. I wasn't even his. One of the girls had me there, and then she just left. My father didn't care whose kid I was. He loved me. He ran a good place. It was a clean place and it was safe and the girls were grateful for it. He protected them. It was a clean place . . ."

Frank said that when his father died, it all fell apart. He didn't have his father's business sense and he was lazy. He didn't fix things and he didn't know everything he had to do to take care of five or six girls. He hadn't paid attention. He was young and stupid. He was only nineteen when he found his father dead of a heart attack in the woods behind the house. His father must have rolled over in his grave the day the place was repossessed by the bank. But it didn't matter. Frank's last girl had already left him, two or three months before.

Frank went to work at Otten's. But the market was still there. All the men who came up to the lake from hundreds of miles away to fish and hunt didn't have to spend their nights alone, if they knew who to call. There were parties in the woods where girls could make a lot of money if they wanted to.

Frank set things up. Protected Tonya and made sure she got paid.

I groaned. "You were her pimp?"

"We were a team, Juney . . ."

Things changed when Tonya got older. Her hair went gray, and she didn't want to dye it.

"She was still so beautiful. With blond hair, she could have passed for twenty-nine. These guys, they know they're not always going to be getting what we tell them they're getting. But they want to be able to pretend," Frank said.

"She wanted out of it. She must have," I said.

"Yeah, but what else were we gonna do?"

Frank said that he would have rather they kept working for themselves. But reality set in. If you were willing to work for someone else, there was another role you could play. The more organized set-ups in Duluth and the Cities were always looking for more girls.

For two weeks, he and Tonya were set up in an apartment in the west end of Duluth. Most of the time, Frank stayed back at the house. Tonya went out looking for girls who needed help. Food. A place to stay.

On the third day, she found Andrea asleep in a bean-bag chair in the children's section of the public library. A runaway from Noka on Ishkode Lake.

Tonya told her that she and her husband were looking for someone to clean their place in exchange for free room and board. For a week, Tonya and Frank cooked spaghetti and hamburgers, Andrea vacuumed and did the dishes.

Once, Tonya left the house for a while so that Frank could be alone with Andrea. He asked her if she wanted to make a little money. He told her that Tonya wouldn't be back for a couple of hours. Frank said he was pretty sure it wasn't the first time Andrea had done that kind of thing for money.

"You're a monster," I said. "You're disgusting. And she was Native American, so that makes it even worse . . ."

"Was she," Frank said glumly, "I didn't know."

"She looked as if she could be. And if she was from Noka . . ."

"You don't know what things are like for these kids, Juney—it's better to let them starve on the street?"

Even Frank knew the wickedness of what they did next. In Ruby's car, he put down his head and worried his fingers together.

They were supposed to be grooming Andrea to work for the organization. Near the end of the two weeks, Frank told Andrea he'd found her another job. She could work a lot more and make a lot more money.

She thought about it, he said. But then she shook her head.

I pictured it. Andrea's polite response, some faint lines working around her small, dark eyes.

"Thanks. But I think I'll stay here," she said.

It was Tonya who was supposed to trick her if she wouldn't go on her own. But Frank told me he hadn't told Tonya this part of the plan in advance. He was sure she wouldn't have agreed to be part of it if she'd known. And he figured he would be able to convince Andrea. Who didn't want to make more money?

The guy they were answering to directly—the blond man from Duluth—suggested that Tonya be the one to orchestrate the ruse. Since she was a woman, and was pretending not to know about Andrea's occasional arrangements with Frank, Andrea would trust her. Would believe her when Tonya said they were just going to a fun party on a boat. As much to eat and drink as they wanted . . .

But when Frank told Tonya, she was furious. No. She wasn't doing that. She had gotten into this on her own volition. She wasn't tricking anyone. Andrea was a sweet kid and she trusted them.

Frank said they had to. This guy would flip out if they didn't follow through. Everyone knew what a psycho he was. Who knew what he'd do if he didn't get what he was paying them for?

Let the guy kill her, then, Tonya said. She wasn't doing it.

She suggested they just try to kick Andrea out. Say that they were sorry, but Tonya and Frank were moving on and they couldn't take Andrea with them. Then they'd tell the maniac Frank had made this devil's agreement with that Andrea had left. Sneaked off in the middle of the night.

The problem was, said Frank, that might be difficult. Andrea thought that living with them was better than both where she'd been before and whatever unknown hell might be ahead. She didn't want to go.

Tonya kept trying to convince Frank. But one morning, she

THE GIRL IN DULUTH

woke up and Andrea was gone. She got out of Frank what he had done; he had never been able to lie to Tonya.

Brought Andrea to the ship party himself. Left her sitting cross-legged on the floor as soon as her eyes started glazing over. Her head drooping over a paper plate of pickles and potato chips.

In the car with me at Hartnell, Frank looked into the rearview mirror and began to talk more quickly. A siren was getting closer.

Tonya didn't sleep at all that night, he said. And it didn't get better when they came back to Aulneau. She couldn't let it go.

It was a done deal, Frank kept telling her. They'd never do it again. Fine. They'd figure something else out. They'd get regular jobs again.

But this—this they just had to leave alone.

No. Tonya wouldn't. She said she was going back to Duluth. She'd ask around and find out what she could. If she knew where Andrea was, maybe she could get her out.

And then what? Frank asked. Whoever had lost Andrea would hunt her down. These guys would be worried that she might say something to the police. They'd resolve to find her first. She'd be as good as dead. That's what happened in these kinds of situations. Frank had seen it a hundred times.

No, said Tonya. She knew some women who used to be in the business, who helped in situations like this.

She asked Frank to come with her. He wouldn't. No, he said. It was suicide. These guys would find out. Then Tonya and Frank would be dead.

Tonya said they would be careful. No one would know it was them. They would make it look as if Andrea had just managed to run away.

Frank reminded Tonya that if she did this, even on her own, and she got caught, they'd think he was involved, too. Is that what she wanted? For Frank to get hunted down and killed?

Over Christmas, Tonya disappeared. When she came back, she wouldn't tell him a thing.

The siren was deafening. Frank kept talking, but I couldn't hear him anymore. I turned around and saw Randy open the door of the white patrol car and get out.

"That's it. You go ahead, Juney," Frank said.

SEVENTEEN

I missed Andrea's funeral. I really did mean to go.

It was held about two weeks later. By that time, Uncle Aaron was back in town. We were packing up all my things and cleaning the apartment. I was running back and forth to the school to talk to my teachers, getting everything set up to finish out the rest of my senior year online from Uncle Aaron's apartment in Minneapolis.

We were wrapping up Tonya's hammers and clamps and my dozens of skirts and sweaters. Carefully carrying the dresser Uncle Rich had made down the stairs and making a judicious decision about leaving the rocking chair and the fifteen-year-old mattresses behind.

I gave most of Tonya's potted herbs to Zee's mother. At the last minute, I decided to keep a couple. The chamomile and the oregano. Uncle Aaron said that this winter he was going to teach me how to make his famous pizza sauce.

In the days after Frank was arrested, I started making searches online to find out about funeral services for Andrea. There were only seven hundred people in Noka. I didn't think it would be that hard.

I couldn't find anything. Finally, I asked Britta and Jack for help. They dug around and found out the problem: Andrea was from Giiwe, not Noka. They were both on the Ishkode Lake reservation, but on different sides of the lake. It wasn't unusual,

Jack said, for these kids to take steps to keep their real origins quiet.

Then I was able to find Andrea's obituary page. I could hardly bear to look at it. There were some blurry baby and childhood pictures that looked exactly like her; her round face and quiet eyes had hardly changed at all. I jotted down the information about her service and created an announcement saying that I was lighting a candle. Then I realized we'd packed all the candles already.

I lit a match and let it burn a second, before blowing it out.

I remembered Tonya's incense, still in the top drawer of her nightstand. We were going to break the stand down and bring Uncle Rich the wood. I didn't like the sharp, musky smell of the only kind of incense she had in there. I lit a cone anyway and let the elegant tendril of black smoke stink up the place.

I tried but couldn't think of anything appropriate to write on Andrea's tribute wall, where some former classmates and her seventh-grade art teacher were speaking about her kindness.

She was fifteen years old. As of today—January 11, 2019—a number of people have been arrested in her case for trafficking and rape. Insufficient evidence has made it difficult to identify which particular individual in that inhuman network shot her down and left her to bleed to death on the street.

On her obituary page, I looked at the option for planting a tree in her honor, but you needed a credit card.

Finally, I closed the tab. But I kept thinking about her, wondering what I could do. I had thought that finding her memorial page might make a path forward on that objective clearer to see and follow. It hadn't.

I checked my email to distract myself. In my inbox was a curious message.

APPLICATION RECEIVED, the subject line said.

It was from a private university in Minneapolis called Augs-

THE GIRL IN DULUTH

burg. Apparently, I had made my official application that very day, January 29, at 3:17 pm?

The past week had been a blur of police interviews and emotional breakdowns, phone calls and life-changing decisions—of many hours spent curled up with a blanket over my head. Every so often I had thought about my college application. Eventually, I had despaired of ever getting to it in time. I gave up. Zee and Uncle Aaron had been right. I should have done it earlier. Now, it was too late.

Except that it appeared I had somehow done it in my sleep . . . I looked at the email for a while. Then I followed the link to "view my application" so I could lay my eyes on the completed version for the first time.

There it was: every line filled in, every box checked. There were even recommendation letters from two teachers. For the essay, "I" had submitted an expertly revised version of an assignment I'd turned in for AP English this past fall.

I sat back in my chair and stared at the screen. How had she done it?

Zee had tweaked the essay for the word count and the prompt. I scanned through it and saw she had also fixed a lot of the more awkward sentences. I would recognize her clever and incisive writing style anywhere.

The revision sounded a hundred times better than my sprawling draft. Why in the world had I been writing for the newspaper all this time, instead of her?

I riled myself up to get angry, because I wanted to be.

I didn't text or call Zee. I did, however, respond to the nudge in the notification email that told me my application wouldn't be 100% complete until I contacted my guidance counselor to get my transcripts transferred.

Uncle Aaron was at the grocery store getting snacks for our trip. He had walked there for the exercise. I didn't have my mother's car back yet—that wouldn't happen for another couple of months—so I grabbed Uncle Aaron's keys from the kitchen counter and drove to school.

After talking to the guidance counselor, I headed to the library on a hunch. I sailed through the halls as I had been doing for the past week, not looking at anyone I passed, kids of driver's license age and above lingering in the halls chatting with one another, taking their time pulling on their jackets and sorting their books just because they could, before ambling to their cars.

I had to remind myself that just a short time ago, I had been one of them. It was hard to believe.

I didn't pretend not to see them, exactly. I just put on my face a purposeful, blazing expression, a shield I knew would be hard to breach.

Zee was just coming out of the computer lab. She was pulling the strap of her messenger bag over her head.

When she saw me, her face went white. For a second, she held the bag in mid-air. Then immediately her skin turned red in blotches. She wiggled her torso like a worm to adjust the strap over her flattened chest, keeping her fingers wrapped tightly around the leather even after it was in place.

She said, "Before you say anything, I'm sorry."

I made her sweat. I stared at her for a minute. "How did you do it?"

"The night you came back from Duluth . . ."

Of course . . . she would have had had time to locate the essay on my computer, email it to herself, and write down my username and password from my notebook, while I was in the bathroom washing the evidence of my lost virginity down the bathtub drain.

"Well." I sighed.

"Do you hate me, or are you glad at all?"

Finally, I smiled. I couldn't help it. The truth was, I was relieved.

I walked up and took her hands. I bent my head towards her, and she did the same. We stood for a while crying quietly a little with our foreheads together like that.

How could I not forgive her, when I was betraying her, too, by leaving her all alone?

"You could stay with me, you know. My parents already said it was all right," Zee had said a few days before, when I told her I was leaving.

In July, when she would come to spend the rest of the summer before she went to college with Uncle Aaron and me, I would ask her tentatively how the rest of the semester had gone.

"How do you think?" she said bitterly.

I let that rest. Then I asked about the kinds of things kids at school had said about me and my mother.

"June." Zee shook her head.

"I want to know. The worst of it. When I go back, I want to know what people are thinking."

"You're going back?"

"I will at some point, right?"

"Most people were nice. They just asked how you were."

"Okay. But—"

"You really want to know?"

I thought about it again. "Yes."

Zee sighed.

"Carter Nordlof told everyone that your mother's pimp came up from the Cities and murdered her in the woods," she said.

However, I digress—I'm getting ahead of myself.

The morning of Andrea's funeral. We were set to leave for Minneapolis the following day, Uncle Aaron and me. The trip from Aulneau to Giiwe took only about an hour and a half. The weather was clear. We had finished packing the night before and we didn't have much more to do.

But I started coming up with excuses. I still had to vacuum

out the back of the closet. I had books and movies to return to the public library and my fee to pay. I should stop by the newspaper office again just to make sure I hadn't left anything there.

Uncle Aaron said, "I already did the closet. And we can run your errands on the way, either today or tomorrow. If we leave today by three, we'll have plenty of time to get to the funeral."

"Yes, but Britta will want to talk. Cindi at the library, too. I hate to just run out without . . ."

Uncle Aaron sat on the carpet and looked at me. Enid climbed into his lap. "It would be nice if you were there, June."

"You think so? I'm scared to go," I said.

"I'll be there with you."

But what would I say, when people at the funeral in Giiwe saw strangers—*white* strangers—and asked how we knew Andrea?

Tell them that my mother had taken advantage of her misery and lured her into prostitution? That I had driven her out of the place she was safe and that was the reason she was dead?

"You can't blame yourself for that. You didn't know. You have to forgive yourself," Uncle Aaron said.

"How could I not have known?" Because, in retrospect, everything seemed so obvious . . .

"You couldn't have. You're only a kid. You didn't have any experience with this kind of thing. Britta, on the other hand," Uncle Aaron said grimly.

"Don't blame Britta. It was Tonya who pulled us all into this."

Uncle Aaron winced. "Can you not call your mom that anymore, June?"

"Call her what?"

"Her name."

I stared at him. "Are you kidding me? She always wanted me to use her name."

"I know that. But now—you don't have to."

"No. I don't *have* to. But maybe I want to," I added slowly.

Uncle Aaron rubbed his forehead with the heel of his hand. Enid's tail ran over his mouth and he brushed it away. "Please don't. She was your mother. I'm sure now she would want—"

"You don't know that. And even if she did—you know," I said, "for all your talk about forgiveness, you're not exactly a good role model for it."

"What do you think all this is about? I do forgive your mother."

"Not Britta," I said. "Not Frank."

"Forgive Frank? You forgive *Frank*?"

"I didn't say that. I'm just saying that Tonya isn't blameless, either. And I don't want to forget that."

"Frank got her into it. And in the end, with the girl, she did the right thing . . ."

"No one forced her to do any of this. Even Aunt Sylvi says that."

"Aunt Sylvi and I see things differently. I don't think anyone is a prostitute by choice. And with what happened to Tonya when she was in high school—"

"Aunt Sylvi worked in social services," I said.

Uncle Aaron stopped replying. After a while, he got up and started cleaning the oven, even though I'd already done it the day before.

As I watched him, I thought of telling him everything about that afternoon with Andrea in the café. How it had been me, not Britta, who had manhandled her, trying to get my precious information. That was probably one of Andrea's last ever interactions with another person, too. Every time I thought of it, my face got hot and I got sick to my stomach.

I couldn't tell him. As much as I complained about Uncle Aaron making excuses for me, I felt I wouldn't be able to bear it if he stopped.

I left the apartment and drove Uncle Aaron's car to school.

I knew when Ms. Karbo had her prep hour. She was in her classroom, packing up dissection tools in the biology lab. For a while, I just helped her without saying much.

Then I told her my problem about the funeral. I told her what I had done to Andrea, too. Ms. Karbo didn't say anything for a few minutes. Then she looked at me, the lines around her eyes deeper than I'd seen them before. She said, "I think you should go to the service, June."

I tried not to look sulky. "Are you sure? What if they don't want me there?"

"Call the director at the funeral home. Explain the situation. Be as honest as you were with me. Ask if he thinks you would be welcome."

"I don't know if I can do that. What if he says no?"

"Well, then, you'll have your answer."

"But I'd feel so bad." I was a little surprised at Ms. Karbo. She was my teacher. She was supposed to protect me. I already felt so awful; I couldn't even imagine how I'd feel after a phone call like that. My mother had just died!

"Couldn't you do it for me?" I said.

Ms. Karbo leaned back against one of the lab tables. She crinkled her brown eyes and crossed her arms and ankles. She had such a sweet, round, motherly face that usually she put off the vibe of a kindergarten teacher rather than a high-school one. But right now, Ms. Karbo looked more like a judge or a prosecuting attorney.

"Now, why would you ask me that?" she said.

I trembled a little under her gaze. I said softly, "Because you're . . ." I didn't have to finish.

"I'm surprised at you, June. That's really disrespectful. And I'm not even Ojibwe—my family is from the Dakota Oyate Nation."

"I'm sorry."

"I'm not going to call for you. You need to do this. And not just for Andrea. It will help you make amends and heal," Ms. Karbo said, speaking more gently again.

"Okay. I'll do it," I said.

On the way home, I thought about what Ms. Karbo had said about healing. I was thinking, too, about a high-school basketball game I'd been to at Ishkode Lake, a long time ago, when I was eleven or twelve. Tonya and Frank had taken me. Before the game started, a small group of men and one boy not much older than I was drummed and sang a flag song in the school gymnasium. They sat in a circle around a big tan drum and hit it with sticks. One of the men would hold his throat when he was reaching for the high notes.

Beside me, Tonya, sitting up very straight on the bleacher, her long hair falling in waves down her back, her hands on her hips, her elbows stuck out straight, was unabashedly happy. She listened closely and closed her eyes to the music.

I was happy, too. And not only because my mother was so full of joy. Even though I couldn't understand the words, I thought it was one of the most beautiful things I'd ever heard. Much of the time, I thought I was going to cry.

Now, looking back at the memory, I wondered if this made me a Pretendian, too.

The rest of the day, Uncle Aaron and I puttered around the apartment, doing mostly nothing. I didn't call the funeral director. The hour of Andrea's service came and went. Its passing didn't give me any relief.

We left early in the morning. As we were driving out of town, I could not summon up the flood of emotion I was expecting. That would come later.

I did feel a gradual loosening of a knot of fear inside me. I was going somewhere where no one knew me or anything about my family. I could walk down the streets in perfect anonymity.

All things considered, we had a nice winter and spring together, Uncle Aaron and me. We went on walks in the snowy city parks and out to concerts and restaurants. I had always thought it was exciting, being in the city, but it had intimidated me as well. Now that I knew I was going to be there for a while, I started to feel less afraid and settled in.

Uncle Aaron was sad about Tonya. But he was also happy. He had kept a second bedroom all this time with almost nothing in it. Now, we fixed it up together. He fussed over me until I had to tell him to stop. I didn't really mind it, though.

We went over to see Aunt Sylvi and Uncle Rich often. When we were all together, our grief over Tonya seemed to grow into something both more poignant and easier to carry.

When Uncle Aaron went back to work, I went to the drug store down the street and picked up a pregnancy test. The next day, I went back and got another one. I knew I was going to want a second opinion, no matter what it said.

For a month, I had all the symptoms. My boobs swelled and ached and the pain made it hard to get to sleep. I had headaches all the time. I was tired, and many mornings I woke up feeling sick to my stomach. Sometimes I threw up. I read online that psychosomatic symptoms were common when you either really wanted to be pregnant, or dreaded it.

Back in Aulneau, a couple days after I'd taken the morning-after pill, I started doing research online to see how effective it might be because of my weight. I found out that you could also use some types of regular birth control as an emergency method, if you took a few pills all at once. I dug out Tonya's pills in the blue container, looked up the brand, and took four orange pills as instructed.

Still, I worried . . .

I got my period on time. I was hopeful, but I didn't trust it. A week later, I took the first pregnancy test. I made myself wait another week before taking the second. Finally, it was time to call Jack.

"It's all right," I said. "I'm not."

"It would have been all right, you know," he said quietly. "Better than all right. You know that."

I made a little murmur without really saying anything. I didn't know what to say. I didn't want to be cruel to Jack. But I had known almost as soon as I arrived here that I couldn't see myself with him at all.

"Are you thinking of coming back here for the summer?"

"Oh—I don't know yet."

Luckily, my college acceptance letter arrived a few days later. Then it was easy to tell Jack that it made more sense to stay here to get ready for the upcoming semester.

It was nice to have something to plan for. A future I could be sure of. When she arrived in July, Zee was an even better distraction. We had a fun summer. There were so many new things to see and do. During the day, we shopped for our dorm rooms and studied descriptions of classes in our course catalogues. We practiced taking the bus and the train from her college to mine. We both had cars; Zee's father had driven Tonya's car down for me, filled with Zee's books and records, when it was released by the police. But both of us quickly preferred public transportation. The whole city was there to see and hear and talk to.

By the time Zee came, the remnants of my fake pregnancy symptoms had mostly gone away. But all that spring and summer, I continued to have trouble getting to sleep.

My whole life, I had always slept pretty well. Not anymore.

It was pleasant to stay up late in Uncle Aaron's pretty apartment, in the spring doing calculus problems and marking up *Hamlet* at my desk near the window, in the summer reading Agatha Christie novels and looking up occasionally to watch people and cars going past, heading to the colored lights of the bars and cafés nearby. Bursts of live music and drunken squeals spilled out every time anyone opened a door.

But a girl had to go to bed sometime. By the time I turned in each night, at three or four or even five, Zee and Uncle Aaron had already been asleep for hours.

But me? When I closed my eyes and tried to sleep, I thought of Andrea. Even more often than I thought of my mother.

Andrea trudging down the steps of the safe house. Andrea clutching her backpack with her toes, cream and a drip of chocolate on her lip.

Andrea climbing a dark street in Duluth, knowing someone was coming. The police said she was running when she was hit and the shot probably came from a car.

Sometimes I tried to convince myself they might be wrong. Maybe she had been sleeping somewhere—in the alley where she was found. Dreaming of the things that, despite everything that had happened to her, she still dreamed of. Even if it was just a peaceful café with the sunlight coming in.

Someone could have crept up on her quietly in the dark. That would mean she stayed in that dream place forever. Maybe she didn't even hear the shot.

As if that were any better—either way, she was still dead.

As for me—I was going to college in the fall. There were books to read and lectures to devour and boys to flirt with. How fun for me!

Andrea had fifteen years. That's it: fifteen difficult years. A mother and older brother who were heroin addicts, Jack had found out.

Now she had nothing. No present, not even a crappy present to struggle to get out of. No future.

And my mother . . .

My mother. My rotten, vile mother!

Tonya, who could have done for Andrea what she was pretending to do, when she first went to the library and touched her sleeping face.

That's how I imagined it. Tonya's gentle, treacherous fingers on Andrea's wide forehead. Behind them, colorful copies of *The Boxcar Children* and *Goodnight Moon*.

"Hey, honey," Tonya probably said. "Are you okay?"

No. Andrea? She wasn't okay. She needed a safe place to go. Three meals a day. Her own bed to sleep in, that belonged to her and to her alone.

She didn't mind working for it. That was all right. She'd washed dishes before. She didn't mind folding clothes.

Instead, Tonya had done what she had done. I could never be sure Frank was telling the truth about her not knowing the end game in advance.

And after knowing what it was like, herself! To be left helpless and alone, trapped on a dark, cold lake. Attacked by men acting like animals.

I knew she'd been a victim herself. I knew that.

But to think that my mother, whose flesh I had come from, whose blood I shared, could have turned that victimhood into *this*. I couldn't forgive her.

Tonya . . . After she betrayed Andrea, she hadn't liked thinking about what she'd done. Obviously. Good!

So she'd taken the easy way out, and left the mess for me to deal with . . .

In August, Uncle Aaron noticed the way my eyelid started to twitch. The black marks under my eyes.

"You might need to talk to someone," he said to me once in the apartment, when Zee was out.

"I talk to you."

"I mean a professional."

"I'll just say the same things. I don't see how it would be better."

One night I didn't sleep at all. I didn't even try. I was sitting in the living room listening to music playing very low. Watching Enid do her night stalking around the room. Attacking bits of dust and flies.

At one point, Enid leapt from the television set, to a plant stand, to the top of the bookshelf where we kept Tonya's ashes in the biodegradable urn we were hoping wouldn't start disintegrating in the summer sun.

In June, we'd had a family discussion about Tonya's ashes. When Aunt Sylvi suggested we drive up some weekend that month to set them out on the lake, I felt a rush of fear. What was it going to be like, the next time I was in Tree Lake again?

I could see the county's natural beauty more clearly now that I was gone. The vast lake. The weird, lonely bog with its stunted plants and wolves howling. The strange and wild things Tonya had loved so much.

But I also felt as if all of the trauma of January might be waiting for me there. In the windows of the apartment when we drove past it. In every road and rock and tree.

I asked if we could put off doing the ashes. No one fought me on it. They might have been thinking the same thing.

In Uncle Aaron's apartment, Enid crept on top of the brown box with Tonya in it and perched there. She purred and flicked her tail, her green eyes shimmering, like some hideous omen out of Edgar Allen Poe.

I jumped out of my chair to grab her and hugged her to my chest. Then I didn't stop crying until the sun came up.

The next morning, I told Uncle Aaron I wanted to find a therapist. The semester was due to start in just a few weeks, so I made an appointment at Augsburg's Center for Wellness a few days before classes would start.

In the meantime, Uncle Aaron suggested that there was also the principle of atonement. I couldn't do anything to help Andrea now. But maybe I could try doing something to atone in her name. Make something good out of something terrible.

"Like what?"

"Well, I know you're not sure about studying journalism anymore."

THE GIRL IN DULUTH

I'm not a great writer

"I'm not a great writer. It's time to admit it."

"That's not true."

"I'm not as good as Zee."

"Comparing yourself to other people isn't helpful, June. But if you're sure, start thinking about what else you might like to do. What about some kind of public service?"

I liked the idea. Augsburg had a long and storied history of community service and social justice. Political activism. Liberation theology. I decided to major in social work, like Aunt Sylvi.

I liked college a lot. I sang in the choir and played a bit part in the fall play. I learned about cultural relativism and the French revolution and the proper use of a semicolon. I saw Zee at least once or twice a week. During the day, I was happy.

There were still nights when I lay in bed with my head turning, instead of getting any rest. I made tea from Tonya's chamomile. Nothing doing.

I still had so many questions. There was one person I knew who might be able to answer them.

The day Frank was arrested, I had told myself I never had to see him or talk to him again. For a while, that was a relief.

My first fall semester ended. Uncle Aaron and I spent Christmas with Aunt Sylvi and Uncle Rich. On New Year's Day, I woke up knowing I had a whole empty week to get through before I could distract myself with school again.

I figured out how to call Frank in prison. He was ecstatic. He wanted to hear all about how I was doing at school.

Instead, I asked him, "So do you think Tonya got that gun in case she needed it when she went to help Andrea escape?"

Frank sighed. "I guess so."

"Frank. Do you think there's any chance someone else killed Tonya?"

He was quiet for a moment. "No. Not really, Juney."

"But you did think it was possible," I said, "before we found her? You thought that someone might have been looking for her?"

"Well. Yeah."

"William McGuire," I said.

William McGuire—the rather distinguished-sounding name of the blond creep with the stony eyes. He was rotting in a jail cell, too. They got him on a million things.

"Him, or someone he worked for . . ."

"That's why you were afraid when we saw the hunters in the woods. You thought it might be him. That he might be following Tonya?"

"Aw, Juney," Frank said and groaned, "why do you want to live all that over again?"

"On our way out of the woods you tried to confuse me . . . you pretended you were lost. You didn't want me to be able to find that spot again."

"Did I?" said Frank.

"Why? Was that a place you had met this guy before—McGuire?"

"McGuire, there?" Frank cried. "That place? No. That was our place."

I wouldn't let it go. Finally, Frank told me: he and Tonya had bought this land because eventually they wanted to build a place to live on it. Of course, their dreams and plans were somewhat different. Tonya envisioned a commune with like-minded people who wanted, like her, to live off the land. She wanted to eat mushrooms and hazelnuts, live high up in the trees. Forget everything that had happened up until this point in her life and cleanse herself in the woods.

Frank wanted that too—mostly because Tonya wanted it. But he also wondered how the place might pay for itself. He was pitching to Tonya the idea that they revive a business like his father's. He felt that with Tonya's help, he could do it right this time.

But Tonya wouldn't be doing any of the dirty work, Frank assured her. Anyway, they would both be too old for that, by the time they got the money and time together to get the building done.

The land was a secret. Only he and Tonya knew the location. They swore never to show it to anyone else. Even close friends like Ruby didn't know.

"Or me? Especially me," I added in a lower voice.

Frank said hopefully, "How's your uncle doing down there?"

"Why do you think she used it to kill herself? The gun?"

"Jesus, Juney . . ."

"She could have taken pills. She could have just stayed out in the storm and frozen to death. Doesn't that seem more like her?"

Frank said after a while, "Maybe before all this. But after Andrea . . ."

Now it was my turn to be quiet.

"I think she thought she deserved it. To get shot down like a dog," Frank said and moaned.

Frank couldn't take any more; I couldn't, either.

A week later, I called him again.

"You can count to nine," I said. "You must have some idea who he is."

"It's not like that. We weren't exactly keeping records. You've gotta just put this out of your head. Tonya was your mother. And I—"

"What about medical stuff?" I interrupted him. "I should know if my father had cancer or something."

"No, I'm sure there isn't anything like that."

"Oh. Well, if you're *sure*," I said acidly.

When school started again, my Center for Wellness counselor said to me, "Do you think that in focusing on your guilt about Andrea, you might be forgetting something?"

"Like what?"

"You tell me."

I said, "My guilt about my mother."

My guilt about my mother? What did I have to feel guilty about *her* for?

I had told my counselor about the imaginary conversations I had had with Tonya's ghost the day we found her dead. She suggested I do it again.

So I did: "Why did you do it?" I asked Tonya.

"I saw the way you looked at me," she said.

My resentment and anger and fear and disgust. When she didn't have any money and the rent was due.

That wasn't the only thing I felt guilty about. I missed my mother. I did. It was impossible to believe, sometimes, that I would never be in the same room as her again. That she couldn't do any of the things she loved anymore. Cutting a paddle through the lake. Dancing with the trees. The pain of those moments was so impossibly sharp and overwhelming it was nearly unbearable.

At the same time, I knew that while it wasn't better, my life was easier now that she was gone.

At the beginning of this year—our senior year—Zee and I began to make plans to get an apartment together in the summer. It's January now. We'll find a place and sign a lease in July. Whenever we have extra time during the day, we look for jobs so we can pay for it.

At night, I haven't stopped talking to Tonya.

I ask her about the days before her death, when she stopped talking to anyone, even Frank.

What was she doing during that time? Just sitting in the woods? Trying to get up her courage to do what she had decided to do? Or trying to decide whether or not she really wanted to do it?

"Saying goodbye," her ghost says.

What could have stopped her? What text or call from me— what words could I have said?

"I'm sorry," I say. "I'm mad at you. But I'm sorry, too."

"For what?"

"For acting like you weren't good enough."

"Jeez, Juney, take it easy. That's what kids do."

"I did love you. I adored you, in a way . . ."

"Thank you, baby. I loved you, too."

"I mean it. I thought you were funny. And free. I think I was jealous of you sometimes."

"Look for me in the stars!"

"You already said that. In your note," I say desperately.

What else does she have for me? Nothing, for a while, but a bunch of mantras and platitudes.

Until I ask her again, "Why did you do it?"

"I did a terrible thing—"

"You tried to fix it. If everyone who did bad things just killed themselves—"

"Yes. I tried to fix it. But after everything I did, I had to ask myself—wouldn't you be safer if I were dead, Juney?"

It's hard to let myself believe that. Even to entertain the possibility that this could have been part of how her reasoning went.

But every night I think it, it makes me feel a little better. One night I change ghosts, right in the middle of a conversation.

"About what happened to you," I say to Andrea.

Andrea is quiet. Her ghost often clams up when I bring up those ugly memories.

"I'm sorry," I say. "I'm so sorry. I applied today to be a counselor at a school. Maybe, if there's another girl, I'll find her before—"

Andrea cuts me off.

"You should have gone to my funeral," she says.

Well. Now we both need cheering up. I change the subject to all the fun things Zee and I do out in Minneapolis and St. Paul.

Most people don't think this is the nicest time of the year to be in the Cities. Nothing green to make the flat, wide streets more beautiful. The dirty snow. Dodging cars on the streets that shrink inch by inch with every storm.

But Zee and I like it. Walking quickly through the dark January cold with our scarves pulled up. On the busiest blocks, white puffs of breath filling the sidewalks. Zee does dramatic spoken word performances in coffee shops. We play ping-pong and air hockey. We watch student films and shaky oboe recitals. Drink hot coffee in restaurants.

Andrea's ghost sighs.

"I would have liked that," she says.

SIGRID BROWN reads, writes, and stays up too late watching mysteries in St. Paul, Minnesota. Read more about her work and her thoughts about books and the performing arts on Facebook and Goodreads and follow her on Twitter @sigridbrown005.